I0600489

Personals

Book and Lyrics by
**David Crane, Seth Friedman
and Marta Kauffman**

Music by
**William Dreskin, Joel Philip Friedman,
Seth Friedman, Alan Menken, Steven
Schwartz and Michael Skloff**

Original New York stage production by
JOHN-EDWARD HILL   ARTHUR MacKENZIE
JON D. SILVERMAN
in association with
FUJISANKEI COMMUNICATIONS GROUP

A SAMUEL FRENCH ACTING EDITION

SAMUEL FRENCH

FOUNDED 1830
New York Hollywood London Toronto
SAMUELFRENCH.COM

Copyright © 1979, 1985, 1987
by David Crane, Seth Friedman and Marta Kauffman

ALL RIGHTS RESERVED

CAUTION: Professionals and amateurs are hereby warned that *PERSONALS* is subject to a Licensing Fee. It is fully protected under the copyright laws of the United States of America, the British Commonwealth, including Canada, and all other countries of the Copyright Union. All rights, including professional, amateur, motion picture, recitation, lecturing, public reading, radio broadcasting, television and the rights of translation into foreign languages are strictly reserved. In its present form the play is dedicated to the reading public only.

The amateur live stage performance rights to *PERSONALS* are controlled exclusively by Samuel French, Inc., and licensing arrangements and performance licenses must be secured well in advance of presentation. PLEASE NOTE that amateur Licensing Fees are set upon application in accordance with your producing circumstances. When applying for a licensing quotation and a performance license please give us the number of performances intended, dates of production, your seating capacity and admission fee. Licensing Fees are payable one week before the opening performance of the play to Samuel French, Inc., at 45 W. 25th Street, New York, NY 10010.

Licensing Fee of the required amount must be paid whether the play is presented for charity or gain and whether or not admission is charged.

Stock licensing fees quoted upon application to Samuel French, Inc.

For all other rights than those stipulated above, apply to: International Creative Management, 825 Eighth Avenue, New York, NY 10019, and The Shukat Company, Ltd, c/o Liebman & Resnick, Ltd. 159 West 53rd Street, Ste 32C, New York, NY 10019.

Particular emphasis is laid on the question of amateur or professional readings, permission and terms for which must be secured in writing from Samuel French, Inc.

Copying from this book in whole or in part is strictly forbidden by law, and the right of performance is not transferable.

Whenever the play is produced the following notice must appear on all programs, printing and advertising for the play: "Produced by special arrangement with Samuel French, Inc."

Due authorship credit must be given on all programs, printing and advertising for the play.

RENTAL MATERIALS

An orchestration consisting of **Piano/Conductor Score (Acoustic Piano, Yamaha DX-7 Synthesizer) Keyboard II (2 DX-7s, one of which is used as a "bass," or 1 DX-7 and a separate bass player), Reed (Flute, Clarinet, Alto & Tenor Saxophones, Cabasa) Guitar (Electric/Acoustic/Banjo), Percussion and 6 Vocal/Chorus Books** will be loaned two months prior to the production ONLY on the receipt of the Licensing Fee quoted for all performances, the rental fee and a refundable deposit. Please contact Samuel French for perusal of the music materials as well as a performance license application.

No one shall commit or authorize any act or omission by which the copyright of, or the right to copyright, this play may be impaired.
No one shall make any changes in this play for the purpose of production.
Publication of this play does not imply availability for performance. Both amateurs and professionals considering a production are strongly advised in their own interests to apply to Samuel French, Inc., for written permission before starting rehearsals, advertising, or booking a theatre.
No part of this book may be reproduced, stored in a retrieval system, or transmitted in any form, by any means, now known or yet to be invented, including mechanical, electronic, photocopying, recording, videotaping, or otherwise, without the prior written permission of the publisher.

ISBN   978-0-573-68124-0   Printed   in   U.S.A.   #18635

IMPORTANT BILLING AND CREDIT REQUIREMENTS

All producers of PERSONALS *must* give credit to David Crane, Marta F. Kauffman, William K. Dreskin, Joel Phillip Friedman, Seth Friedman, Stephen Schwartz, Michael Skloff and Alan Menken in all programs distributed in connection with performances of the Work, and in all instances in which the title of the Work appears for the purpose of advertising, publicizing or otherwise exploiting the Work and/or a production thereof; including, without limitation, programs, souvenir books and playbills. The names of the Authors *must* also appear on separate lines in which no other matter appears, immediately following the title of the Work, and *must* be in size of type not less than 50% of the size of type used for the title of the Work.

Billing shall be in the following form;
(name of producer)
presents
P E R S O N A L S
Book and Lyrics by
David Crane, Seth Friedman,
Marta Kauffman
Music by
William K. Dreskin, Joel Phillip Friedman, Seth Friedman,
Alan Menken, Stephen Schwartz, Michael Skloff

The Licensee is also required to give credit to the original Producers as follows:

Original New York stage production by
John-Edward Hill, Arthur MacKenzie
and Jon D. Silverman
in association with
Fujisankei Communications Group

MINETTA LANE THEATRE

An M-Square Entertainment Inc. Theatre

JOHN-EDWARD HILL ARTHUR MacKENZIE JON D. SILVERMAN

in association with

FUJISANKEI COMMUNICATIONS GROUP

present

PERSONALS
A MUSICAL REVUE

Written by and Lyrics by

DAVID CRANE, SETH FRIEDMAN, MARTA KAUFFMAN

Music by

WILLIAM DRESKIN, JOEL PHILLIP FRIEDMAN, SETH FRIEDMAN,
ALAN MENKEN, STEPHEN SCHWARTZ, MICHAEL SKLOFF

With
(in alphabetical order)

JASON ALEXANDER   LAURA DEAN   DEE HOTY
JEFF KELLER   NANCY OPEL   TREY WILSON

Scenery by	Costumes by	Lighting by	Sound by
LOREN SHERMAN	ANN HOULD-WARD	RICHARD NELSON	OTTS MUNDERLOH

Musical Director & Vocal Arrangements	Orchestrations	Production Stage Manager
MICHAEL SKLOFF	STEVEN OIRICH	TOM ABERGER

General Management	Casting
WEILER/MILLER ASSOCIATES	McCORKLE CASTING

Choreography by

D.J. GIAGNI

Directed by

PAUL LAZARUS

4

CAST

(in alphabetical order)

Louis & Others .... JASON ALEXANDER
Kim & Others .... LAURA DEAN
Claire & Others .... DEE HOTY
Sam & Others .... JEFF KELLER
Louise & Others .... NANCY OPEL
Typesetter & Others .... TREY WILSON

UNDERSTUDIES

Understudies never substitute for listed players unless a specific an-
nouncement for the appearance is made at the time of the performance.

For Kim, Claire, Louise—Kathryn Morath; for Louis, Sam, Typesetter—Stephen McNaughton.

MUSICAL NUMBERS

ACT I

"Nothing to Do with Love" (music by Stephen Schwartz) .... The Company
"After School Special" (music by William Dreskin) .... Jason & Company
"Mama's Boys" (music by Seth Friedman & Joel Phillip Friedman) .... Dee, Laura,
Trey & Company
"A Night Alone" (music by Michael Skloff) .... Jeff, Jason, Dee, Trey
"I Think You Should Know" (music by Seth Friedman & Joel Phillip Friedman) .. Laura, Jeff
"Second Grade" (music by Michael Skloff) .... Jeff, Jason, Trey & Company
"Imagine My Surprise" (music by William Dreskin) .... Dee
"I'd Rather Dance Alone" (music by Alan Menken) .... The Company

INTERMISSION

ACT II

"Moving in with Linda" (music by Stephen Schwartz) .... Jeff & Company
"A Little Happiness" (music by Seth Friedman & Joel Phillip Friedman) .... Trey
"I Could Always Go to You" (music by Alan Menken) .... Dee, Nancy
"The Guy I Love" (music by William Dreskin) .... Nancy, Jason
"Michael" (music by William Dreskin) .... Laura
"Picking Up the Pieces" (music by Seth Friedman & Joel Phillip Friedman) ... Jason, Trey
"Some Things Don't End" (music by Stephen Schwartz) .... The Company

Lyrics to all songs by David Crane, Seth Friedman, Marta Kauffman.

ORCHESTRA: Conductor / piano / synthesizer — Michael Skloff; Guitars — Gregory Utzig;
Reeds — William Harris; Percussion — Bruce Doctor; Synthesizers — Wayne Abravanel.

5

CAST OF CHARACTERS

3 Women and 3 Men playing various roles as follows:

WOMAN #1, CLAIRE, MARILOU, GROUP MEMBER

WOMAN #2, KIM, ELAINE, GROUP MEMBER

WOMAN #3, LOUISE, TINA, MOTHER #3, RICKI BUSH, FEMALE TAPE VOICE, HANNAH KLEIN, RENE, GROUP MEMBER

MAN #1, SAM, MOTHER #1, GROUP MEMBER

MAN #2, LOUIS, CHUCKIE, MOTHER #2, MOVER, BOB, MR. PO-TATO HEAD

MAN #3, TYPESETTER, MALE TAPE VOICE, TONY LAMBUSCO, MOVER, GROUP MEMBER

ACT ONE

NOTHING TO DO WITH LOVE
Typesetter #1
AFTER SCHOOL SPECIAL
Woman Seeks
Typesetter #2
MAMA'S BOYS
VIDEOMATCH
Videomatch — Tina
Louis #1
A NIGHT ALONE
Videomatch — Ricki
Louis #2
I THINK YOU SHOULD KNOW
Typesetter #3
Videomatch — Hannah
SECOND GRADE
Louis #3
IMAGINE MY SURPRISE
I'D RATHER DANCE ALONE

ACT TWO

MOVING IN WITH LINDA
A LITTLE HAPPINESS
Kim's Monologue
I COULD ALWAYS GO TO YOU
Group
THE GUY I LOVE
MICHAEL
The Meeting Section
PICKING UP THE PIECES
Sam and Claire Scene
SOME THINGS DON'T END

MUSICAL CUES

1   NOTHING TO DO WITH LOVE
1A NOTHING TO DO WITH LOVE – PLAYOFF
2   AFTER SCHOOL SPECIAL
2A WOMAN SEEKS PLAYOFF
3   MAMA'S BOYS
4   VIDEOMATCH
4A TINA PLAYOFF
5   A NIGHT ALONE
5A INTO RICKI BUSH
5B OUT OF RICKI BUSH
6   I THINK YOU SHOULD KNOW
6A HANNAH KLEINE NEXTMUSIK
7   SECOND GRADE
7A GRADE B PLAYOFF
8   IMAGINE MY SURPRISE
9   I'D RATHER DANCE ALONE

10 MOVING IN WITH LINDA
10A LINDA PLAYOFF
11 A LITTLE HAPPINESS
11A KIM'S PLAYOFF
12 I COULD ALWAYS GO TO YOU
12A GROUP I
12B GROUP II
13 THE GUY I LOVE
14 MICHAEL
15 MEETING SECTION
15A PICKING UP LOUIS
16 PICKING UP THE PIECES
16A TO SAM AND CLAIRE SCENE
17 FINALE (SOME THINGS DON'T END)
18 BOWS (NOTHING TO DO WITH LOVE REPRISE)

Personals

ACT ONE

As the audience enters, they see an enormous reproduction of a page of personal ads on the show drop.

The stage goes to black. A pinspot picks out an ad on the drop:

Real fine lookin' one-legged lady wishes to know tight one-legged man. Box 619

The spotlight travels to another ad:

Single white grandmother, 70 and holding, seeks Heathcliff. Box 423

The spot moves on to:

All I need is a good man and a good piano. I've got a good piano. Box 1201

[MUSIC NO. 1: NOTHING TO DO WITH LOVE]

The piano music begins. The curtain opens. The ACTORS are seated, holding various notepads and papers, except for KIM, who stands facing upstage.

NOTHING TO DO WITH LOVE

KIM. (*turning to face the audience, newspaper in hand*) There it is. That's me on that page. That's my ad. Now I'd answer that ad. I would. And then I'd get to meet me and I'd fall for me like that. (*Pause.*) I hope I'm not the *only* one to answer this ad.
SAM. (*looking up*)
FIFTEEN WORDS
TWO LINES
RUNNING FOR THREE WEEKS.
STARTING WITH "SINGLE MALE SEEKS."
KIM.
TWENTY-SIX WORDS

9

FOUR LINES
KIND OF COY AND SORT OF FORCED.
STARTS WITH "RECENTLY DIVORCED."
(*KIM crosses toward SAM.*)
  BOTH.
ENDS WITH
  KIM.
"NO BOZOS . . ."
  SAM.
"NO BIMBOS . . ."
  BOTH.
"PLEASE."
I CAN'T BELIEVE I'M DOING ONE OF THESE.

(*CLAIRE has been sitting on the* D.R. *platform; she stands.*)

  CLAIRE. A recent study entitled: "Single in the City", has determined that although I am bright, attractive, and unusually self-aware, I live alone, lead a limited social life and approach everything with an extremely defensive attitude. They conclude that there is little I can do to alter my situation and in all likelihood I am unhappy. For this they spent six years and five million dollars in government grants. They could have just asked me!!! (*She sits.*)
  WOMAN #3.
FORTY-TWO WORDS
ALL BOLD
COST ME EIGHTY SEVEN BUCKS.
TURNING THIRTY REALLY SUCKS.
  MAN #2.
TWO HUNDRED SIXTY TWO WORDS
TOO LONG
AND MUCH TOO PERFECT TO BELIEVE.
SO I'LL STAY HOME ON NEW YEAR'S EVE.
  MAN #3.
FORTY-SIX WORDS
TOO STRONG.
  CLAIRE.
THIRTY-NINE WORDS
TOO TRITE.
  SAM.
TWENTY-EIGHT WORDS
ALL WRONG.

ALL.
FIFTEEN WORDS (FIFTEEN WORDS) (FIFTEEN WORDS)
ALRIGHT!!

(*All the ACTORS stand. CLAIRE's chair rolls off* R. *on platform. SAM's chair is pulled off* L.)

ALL. (*continued*)
THIS HAS NOTHING TO DO WITH LOVE.
THIS HAS EVERYTHING TO DO WITH JARGON.
NOTHING TO DO WITH LOVE.
THIS HAS MOSTLY TO DO
WITH A STRONG PITCH
AND A SMOOTH SELL
AND A BARGAIN.

THIS HAS NOTHING TO DO WITH LOVE.
THIS HAS QUITE A LOT TO DO WITH GRAMMAR.
NOTHING TO DO WITH LOVE.
THIS HAS SOMETHING TO DO
WITH A SQUARE PEG
AND A ROUND HOLE
AND A HAMMER.

BUT I KNOW THERE'S SOMEONE OUT THERE,
WAITING SOMEWHERE IN THE NIGHT,
SOMEONE WAITING FOR MY FIFTEEN WORDS
TO LIGHT UP THE BLACK AND WHITE.
AND ALL I GOTTA DO IS GET 'EM RIGHT!

(*The three MEN appear, as in a dream.*)

MAN #3.
"Sensitive poet/millionaire with body like statue of David seeks woman to share his Greek island."

WOMEN. (*over the dialogue*)
OOO . . .

MAN #1.
"Successful architect/neurosurgeon/and heir to the throne of small European country seeks woman to give meaning to a life of superficial perfection."

WOMAN. (*over the dialogue*)
OHHHH . . .

MAN #2.   WOMEN. (*over the dialogue*)
"Virtual demi-god and Lord of AHHHH . . .
small planet seeks woman to
share his myth."

(*The LIGHTS change.*)

ALL.
THIS HAS NOTHING TO DO WITH LOVE.
THIS HAS MORE AND MORE TO DO WITH DICTION.
NOTHING TO DO WITH LOVE.
THIS HAS MOSTLY TO DO
WITH A QUICK TURN
OF A CUTE PHRASE
 MEN.
AND A KNACK FOR FICTION.

 ALL.
BUT I KNOW THERE'S SOMEONE OUT THERE,
WAITING SOMEWHERE IN THE NIGHT,
SOMEONE WAITING FOR MY FIFTEEN WORDS
TO LIGHT UP THE BLACK AND WHITE.
(*MAN #2 has put glasses on during the previous verse; he steps forward.*)
 LOUIS (MAN #2).
AND I THINK THIS TIME I FINALLY GOT IT RIGHT:
"Hello. My name is Louis. Would you have dinner with me?"
(*Pause.*) That's it.
 WOMAN #3. "Pre-owned woman with good body and mileage, wants man. Not sure why."
 MAN #3. "Beat me. Whip me. Gag me. Tie me down. Hurt me, hurt me. Nothing is too humiliating. (*Pause.*) Relationship must be based on quiet understanding and mutual respect."
 CLAIRE. "This is my first and last ad. Woman who embodies the usual list of qualities is looking for a man who normally wouldn't answer one of these things."
 ALL. (*in canon*)
FIFTEEN WORDS . . .
 WOMAN #1.
SENSUOUS EXECUTIVE
 ALL.
FIFTEEN WORDS . . .

Man #1.
BLUE-EYED CAPRICORN
All.
FIFTEEN WORDS . . . (FIFTEEN WORDS)
Woman #3.
NEVER BEEN IN THERAPY
All.
FIFTEEN WORDS
FIFTEEN WORDS
FIFTEEN WORDS
Women.
WHILE YOU WAIT FOR YOUR PRINCE TO COME
Man #1.
JEWISH AND SENSITIVE
Man #3, Woman #1.
HEALTHY REPUBLICAN
Man #2.
NO MISS AMERICAS
Woman #3.
MUST LOVES ANIMALS
(*Following lines through* DESPERATE *overlap.*)
Woman #2.
MY MOTHER THINKS I'M BRIGHT AND BEAUTIFUL
Woman #1, Woman #3.
STOP! YOU'VE FOUND HER
Men.
SWINGING
PSYCHIC
WITTY
HORNY
LONELY
DESPERATE
All.
THIS HAS NOTHING TO DO WITH LOVE
THIS HAS EVERYTHING TO DO WITH
BLIND DATES
Man #1, Woman #2.
LONELY NIGHTS
All.
BLIND DATES
SINGLES BINGO
Woman #3.
T.V. DINNERS

ALL.
BLIND DATES
  MAN #3.
MY WIFE'S LOVER
  MAN #2.
MY MOTHER'S NAGGING
  ALL.
AND PUSH FINALLY COMING TO SHOVE
THIS HAS NOTHING TO DO WITH,
EVERYTHING TO DO WITH,
NOTHING TO DO WITH LOVE! ·

(*At the end of the song, all the ACTORS sit on the 3 remaining
    chairs, 2 people per chair. Blackout. The ACTORS exit with
    chairs and handprops.*)

[MUSIC NO. 1A: NOTHING TO DO WITH LOVE — PLAYOFF]

* * *

TYPESETTER #1

*LIGHTS up on MAN #3 (TYPESETTER), as the Typesetter
    platform rolls on from* S.R. *He puts on visor, sits at the desk,
    and begins typing. He reads from what he is typing:*

TYPESETTER. "Refined gentleman seeks marriage with very
hairy woman. All sizes considered." (*He looks up from what he
is doing and speaks to the audience.*)
    I've been typing these things here at the paper for 15 years
now, and if you want an expert's opinion: I think they're silly. My ·
wife, Adelle, on the other hand, thinks they're disgusting. I tell
her she's taking them too seriously. She says they're vulgar and
degrading. I tell her she's getting carried away. She says she'd
sooner die than subject herself to this sort of public humiliation.
It would kill her. It would just kill her. (*Beat.*) I figured it was
worth a shot. (*He reads from a little card on his desk:*)
    "Seeking bisexual transvestite dwarf for possible long term
commitment. Meet me outside the Holland Tunnel at midnight
on Christmas Eve dressed as Carmen Miranda in 'That Night in
Rio'. You just might be the dwarf of my dreams. Kisses,
Adelle." (*He smiles and shrugs.*)

If she dies, she dies. (*He resumes typing, as his platform rolls off* R.)

* * *

AFTER SCHOOL SPECIAL

[MUSIC NO. 2]

CHUCKIE (MAN #2) runs on from up L. *He smiles innocently at the audience and sings:*

MAN #2.
I NEVER DID IT.
I JUST NEVER DID IT.
I WANTED TO DO IT.
I'D WAITED SO LONG.
I'D READ ALL ABOUT IT
I KNEW I COULD DO IT,
IF SOMEONE WOULD LET ME,
IF NOTHING WENT WRONG.

IT SOUNDED TERRIFIC
AND I'D SEEN A FEW PICTURES.
MY FRIENDS HAD ALL DONE IT,
THEY SWORE THAT THEY HAD.
IN A MOMENT OF PANIC
WHEN NO ONE WAS LOOKING,
I MADE A DECISION,
I TOOK OUT THIS AD:

HIGH SCHOOL SENIOR
NEEDS A TEACHER
FOR A PARTICULAR
EXTRA-CURRICULAR.
YOU'D BE MY FIRST
IF YOU KNOW WHAT I MEAN.
COULD SOMEONE PLEASE HELP A NEEDY TEEN?

I SAW IT IN PRINT
AND IT SUDDENLY HIT ME
WHAT IF THE PERSON WHO ANSWERED WAS WEIRD?

KINDA SADISTIC?
OR HAD AN INFECTION?
OR LOOKED LIKE MRS. MULLER
WITH HER MAKE-UP ALL SMEARED?

IT WAS 10:47
THE MAILMAN WAS COMING,
10:48
HE STOOD IN THE HALL,
AND AT 10:49
A VOICE DEEP INSIDE ME
SAID: "CHUCKY,
YOU MIGHT GET LUCKY . . .
AND GET NO RESPONSE AT ALL."

WHEN HE REACHED INTO THE MAILBAG
MY HEART WENT THROUGH THE FLOOR,
THERE WASN'T A SINGLE RESPONSE . . .
THERE WERE ONE HUNDRED AND NINETY-FOUR.

(*As MAN #2 continues, the CAST sing back-up on offstage mic.*)

AND I ANSWERED EVERY LETTER
LIKE EACH ONE WAS THE FIRST,
I'VE BEEN RUNNING THAT SAME AD NOW FOR A YEAR!
AND MY SKIN KEEPS GETTIN' CLEARER
EVERY WEEK THESE WORDS APPEAR:

    MAN #2 and ALL.
HIGH SCHOOL SENIOR
NEEDS A TEACHER
FOR A PARTICULAR
EXTRA-CURRICULAR.
YOU'D BE MY FIRST
IF YOU KNOW WHAT I MEAN.
COULD SOMEONE PLEASE HELP A NEEDY TEEN?

HIGH SCHOOL SENIOR
NEEDS A TEACHER
FOR A PARTICULAR
EXTRA-CURRICULAR.
YOU YOU YOU YOU'D BE MY FIRST

IF YOU KNOW WHAT I MEAN.
COULD SOMEONE PLEASE HELP A NEEDY TEEN?
(HIGH SCHOOL SENIOR
NEEDS A TEACHER.)
    MAN #2.
HELP A NEEDY TEEN!
(*He exits.*)

* * *

WOMAN SEEKS

"Videomatch panel" flies in. KIM enters from upstage R. and crosses to downstage center of panel.

KIM. Attractive woman, recently divorced after five years of uneventful marriage, is extremely curious to discover what's out there. Seeks good-looking, fun loving man who will show her what she's been missing. No bozos, please.

(*MAN #3 enters from upstage R. and crosses to her.*)

MAN #3. Good-looking, fun-loving man seeks slender and sensuous female for discreet afternoon discoveries.

(*She moves to him. They begin to play a game, turning each other on. Each lines tops the last:*)

KIM. Slender and sensuous female seeks passionate, imaginative male for weekends of shared delights.
MAN #3. Passionate, sun-starved male seeks uninhibited female for skinny dipping and other wet erotica.
KIM. New-found nudist seeks wonderfully athletic male for sun-bathing on hot rocks.
MAN #3. Hot male seeks furry feline for heavy petting.
KIM. Lustful lioness dares ferocious lion to play in her den.
MAN #3. Well equipped animal seeks sensational partner for relentless mating.
KIM. Sensational partner seeks well equipped animal with eight inches of power.
MAN #3. Well equipped animal with nine inches —
KIM. Ten inches.
MAN #3. Twelve inches.

KIM. Twelve inches? (*This is more than she is prepared to handle. She turns away.*) Woman seeks man friend for more conservative arrangement.

(*MAN #3 exits upstage of the Videomatch panel. MAN #2 enters with clipboard from the left of the panel and crosses to her.*)

MAN #2. Successful professional man seeks pleasant compatible woman for meaningful relationship.

KIM. Expressive—

MAN #2. (*cutting her off*) For *serious* meaningful relationship.

KIM. For—

MAN #2. For possible *long term* serious meaningful relationship.

KIM. For—

MAN #2. Children okay.

KIM. Children?

MAN #2. Only those pleasant compatible women with a genuine interest in marriage need apply.

(*She moves away from MAN #2, who then exits upstage L.*)

KIM. *Independent* woman, recently *divorced*, seeks something new and different.

(*MAN #1 enters from right of panel, crosses to her and grabs her shoulder.*)

MAN #1. Self-destructive hunchback with all-consuming lingerie fetish desires satin soft creatures for midnight experiments. (*KIM shudders.*)

KIM. Woman seeks simple, down-to-earth relationship.

(*MAN #1 exits left of panel then re-enters right of panel.*)

MAN #1. Simple, down-to-earth guy seeks kind and sensitive woman who will help preserve the tenuous grasp on reality it has taken him years to develop. (*He takes her hand.*) Who will not be manipulative and hostile, forcing him ever closer to the black abyss that yawns before his feet . . .

(*He totally withdraws. She pulls her hand away, and growing in-*

creasingly desperate, continues speaking. MAN #1 exits
stage R. *of panel.*)

KIM. Woman seeks mature, good natured man strong enough
to handle his own problems.

(*MAN #2 enters stage* L. *of panel; pulls her to him.*)

MAN #2. Mature, good natured man, strong enough to handle
anything, seeks slaves for dominance training. Straps, whips,
belts, knuckles, buckles, paddles, prongs: anything goes!

(*MAN #3 enters* R. *of panel.*)

MAN #3. Man has done it all: Leather, chains, S&M, B&D —
KIM. (*getting fed up*) Look, woman is strictly M&M's and
T.V. and occasionally the A&P, so —
MAN #3. But has she ever done G&S?

(*MAN #2, horrified, exits* L. *of panel.*)

KIM. (*in spite of herself*) G&S?
MAN #3. (*enthusiastically*) You wanna talk about *pain*? Some
of the most tedious operettas you have ever heard: "Iolanthe",
"The Gondoliers", "Yoeman of the Guard" — (*He begins to hum
a Gilbert & Sullivan tune.*)
KIM. No! Woman is only looking to get involved in a solid,
secure, loving relationship.

(*MAN #1 appears left of panel.*)

MAN #1. I'm crazy about my wife, and I think you will be,
too. Come join us in our — (*MAN #2 enters left of panel.*) —
luxurious penthouse apartment with a breathtaking view of Cen-
tral Park . . .

(*KIM turns to MAN #2. MAN #1 continues, overlapping.*)

KIM. Woman seeks —
MAN #2. Family-minded man seeks unmarried woman to
carry his child. $10,000 now and another $10,000 upon proof of
conception . . . (*MAN #2 also continues.*)
KIM. Woman seeks —

MAN #3. Ever considered animal husbandry? Old MacDonald had a farm. Eee-eye-eee-eye-oh! With an oink oink here and an oink oink there . . .

(*ALL are speaking at once, moving toward her. Their voices build and build, until:*)

KIM. HELP!! (*ALL stop.*) Attractive woman, recently divorced, seeks well-rounded relationship. (*The MEN exit indignantly.*) No bozos. *Please.*

(*KIM staggers off, right.*)

* * *

[MUSIC NO. 2A: WOMAN SEEKS — PLAYOFF]

TYPESETTER #2

The platform with Typesetter setup rolls on from stage R. As the Videomatch panel flies out, the TYPESETTER (MAN #3) crosses to meet the platform and the lights crossfade.

TYPESETTER. (*carefully*) We're driving home from my sister's in Jersey, and just as we stop to pay the toll, Adelle nudges me and points. I look over and I can barely make out this little figure huddled in the snow wearing a strapless gown and fruit in his hair. That's when I remember. I tell you, I just didn't have the heart to drive on.

We get out of the car and go over to him. The dwarf looks up at us. He's shivering. So I explain about the ad and how it was all a joke . . . well he starts to cry. I turn to Adelle and she's in shock. The little guy is shaking now and making these hiccuppy noises and, Christ, I don't know what to say. All of a sudden he throws his maracas on the ground and runs into the tunnel. Well, we had to go after him. (*He looks down, embarrassed.*)

Anyway, Mr. Blini's been living with us for about a week now. He pretty much keeps to himself and, well, I just figured we had to do something, you know? I had no idea people might actually answer these things.

(*He exits R. and the Typesetter platform rolls off R.*)

* * *

MAMA'S BOYS

[MUSIC NO. 3]

MUSIC begins. WOMAN #1 is on the phone downstage L.

WOMAN #1. Mother, I'm not going. (*Pause.*) I'm sure he's a nice boy, but . . . Mother, may I speak? (*Long pause.*) Mother, I am not going to Rose Siegel's funeral just to meet her son. That's it!

(*WOMAN #2 and MAN #1 enter.*)

WOMAN #1. (*continued*) Of course I love you. Look, I gotta go! (*WOMAN #1 hangs up and crosses center with a microphone. She steps forward and sings.*)
HE WAS CHIEF
OF OB/GYN AT MOUNT SINAI.
  WOMAN #2 & MAN #3.
(SINAI)
  WOMAN #1.
MY MOTHER MET HIM
BY THE POOL OF THE FOUNTAINBLEU.
  WOMAN #2 & MAN #3.
(OOH . . .)
  WOMAN #1.
SHE WROTE MY NUMBER ON A NAPKIN
SAID TO GIVE ME A BUZZ,
  WOMAN #2 & MAN #3.
(SHA LA LA LA LA)
  WOMAN #1.
THE NEXT DAY
I OPENED MY DOOR, AND THERE HE WAS:
HE WAS SHORT,
HE WAS BALD,
HE WAS MIDDLE AGED.
IN A MONTH
WE WERE ENGAGED.

  ALL.
HE WAS
ONE OF THE MEN
MY MOTHER MADE ME LOVE.

MY MOTHER MADE ME LOVE.
  WOMAN #1.
MY MOTHER MADE ME . . . LOVE.
  WOMAN #2.
HE WAS OUT
AFTER SERVING THREE TO FIVE
AT RIKER'S ISLAND
  WOMAN #1 & MAN #3.
(ISLAND.)
  WOMAN #2.
MY MOTHER MET HIM
  WOMAN #1 & MAN #3.
(SHE MET HIM)
  WOMAN #2.
WHEN I BROUGHT HIM TO MY SWEET SIXTEEN.
  WOMAN #1 & MAN #3.
(SWEET SIXTEEN)
  WOMAN #2.
SHE PUT HER HEAD INTO THE OVEN
  WOMAN #1 & MAN #3.
(OOH . . .)
  WOMAN #2.
SAID SHE WANTED TO DIE.
  WOMAN #1 & MAN #3.
(SHA LA LA LA LA)
  WOMAN #2.
THAT'S WHEN I KNEW
HE WAS MY KIND OF GUY:
  WOMAN #1 & MAN #3.
(OOOH — MY KIND OF GUY)
  WOMAN #2.
HE WAS CRASS,
HE WAS CRUDE,
HE WAS HUMAN DEBRIS.
THREE YEARS OF ANALYSIS HELPED ME TO SEE

  ALL.
HE WAS
ONE OF THE MEN
MY MOTHER MADE ME LOVE.
MY MOTHER MADE ME LOVE.
  WOMAN #2.
MY MOTHER MADE ME LOVE.

DON'T GET ME STARTED ON MY M-M-M-MOTHER.
THERE IS NOTHING I CAN DOOO . . .
THE ONLY JUSTICE
IS MY M-M-M-M-MOTHER
HAS GOT A M-M-M-MOTHER, TOO-OO-OO.

(*There is a short dance break, at the end of which MAN #1 steps forward and sings.*)

MAN #1.
HE WAS GOLD
OF GOLD, LEVINE, LEVEEN, AND BENIDETTO.
    WOMAN #1. Good firm.
    MAN #1.
MY MOTHER MET HIM
SAID HE WAS PERFECT FOR MY SISTER RUTH.
    WOMEN. Did you say he was perfect for your sister Ruth?
    MAN #1.
NO ONE COULD TELL HER
THE OBVIOUS TRUTH.
    WOMAN #2. What was that?
    MAN #1.
SHE FOUND A CATCH, ALRIGHT
BUT NOT FOR RUTH:
    BOTH WOMEN. Unh uh.
    MAN #1.
HE WAS TALL,
HE WAS SMART,
HE WAS SOCIALLY GRACED.
THANK GOD FOR MOM'S IMPECCABLE TASTE.

(*A platform rolls on from stage R. with 3 "MOTHERS" [WOMAN #3, MEN #1 & #2] playing Mah Jong and eating potato chips. They talk in the background during the chorus.*)

ALL.
HE WAS ONE
OF THE MEN
MY MOTHER MADE ME LOVE
WHOA THE MEN
MY MOTHER MADE ME LOVE
YES SHE DID

MY MOTHER MADE ME LOVE
OOH OOH
MY MOTHER MADE ME . . .

MOTHER #1. (*during the chorus*) I can't talk about it. Charlotte, that child is going to send me to an early grave.

MOTHER #2. I know. Don't I know?

MOTHER #3. They're married six months and she leaves him. And he's a dentist, no less.

MOTHER #1. And not bad looking at all.

MOTHER #3. What is that child thinking?

MOTHER #2. I know. Don't I know?

MOTHER #3. Last week, my Cindy brings home a convict. Lydia, you could still see the manacle marks on his wrists.

(*The singing stops.*)

MOTHER #1. (*In the break:*) "There's no magic", she tells me. You want magic, marry the Amazing Kreskin.

(*The MUSIC starts again.*)

MOTHER #2. Believe me, I *know*. I said to my Gail the other day, "Baby, it's not like you're 18 anymore." My god, the girl's amost 24!

MOTHERS #1, #3. Boys! We should have had only boys!

MOTHER #2. I know. Don't I know?

(*All three MOTHERS ad lib until scream:*)

WOMAN #2, #1 and MAN #1.
M-M-M-M-M-M-M-M-M-M-M-(*The MUSIC builds harmonically to a vocal scream.*) M-M-M-M-M-M-M-M-M-AGGG-GGHHHH!

MOTHER #1. What, did I say something?

ALL.
HE WAS ONE
OF THE MEN
MY MOTHER MADE ME LOVE! (LOVE THE MEN)
MY MOTHER MADE ME
LOOOOOOOOOVE
LOOOOOOOOOVE
M-M-M-M-M-M-THE MEN . . .

Man #3. (*falsetto*)
MY MOTHER MADE ME LOVE!
All.
LOVE!!

(*Blackout.*)

* * *

VIDEOMATCH

[MUSIC NO. 4: VIDEOMATCH]

*In the darkness we hear a tacky commercial jingle. The Video-
match panel flies in.*

Offstage Singers (Woman #2, Man #1).
HAVING TROUBLE FINDING THAT SPECIAL
    SOMEONE?   (SOMEONE)
HAVING TROUBLE HOOKING THAT PERFECT CATCH?
SEE WHAT YOU'RE GETTING BEFORE YOU GET STUCK
    Woman's Voice (Woman #2). (*spoken*) I can't believe my
luck!
    Offstage Singers.
THE BEST IN THE CITY,
IT'S VIDE-O-
MATCH.
    Woman's Voice (Woman #2). Natch'!

VIDEOMATCH—TINA

(*CLAIRE [WOMAN #1] enters stage R. with a modern chrome
chair and a clipboard. She crosses behind the panel and
brings on TINA [WOMAN #3]. TINA is high-strung and
more than a little nervous.*)

Claire. Hi, Tina, I'm Claire. Now have a seat right here.
When you see that red light go on, you'll have 30 seconds to say
whatever you want. Just be yourself, because that's the you they
want to see. Any questions?
    Tina. I thought I'd start by explaining why I'm doing this.
    Claire. That sounds fine.

TINA. And then I'll discuss what I'm looking for in a relationship.

CLAIRE. When the light comes on.

TINA. And then I'm going to talk about my good qualities. I thought I'd do good qualities last because I know you want to leave them with a good impres—(*A bright white light comes on TINA. She speaks to the camera:*)

Hello. I'm Tina. Number One: Why am I doing a thing like this? Well it all started this morning. On my face. A wrinkle. My first. Can you see it? It's right over here. Now I know it's not much, and you'd probably call it a "laugh line", but I'm sorry, things haven't been that funny. See, I know what this is. It's the beginning. Of the end. It's the beginning of the end. Sure there's just one now, but pretty soon there'll be two, then three, then my hair'll turn grey, then blue, and then it'll fall out. And I'll shrink and lose all my teeth. And I'll get chicken skin . . . here. And here. Then my ankles will get fat and hang over the tops of my shoes . . . (*She is out of the chair, a snowball down a mountain.*) And I'll spend all afternoon in Gristedes saying, "Graham crackers." I'll say, "Graham crackers. Where are the Graham crackers?!" And who's going to want me then, huh? Nobody! So that's why I'm doing this now before it's too late!!!! (*Beat. She slowly sits, trying to regain her composure.*)

Number Two: What I'm looking for in a relationship—

CLAIRE. (*cutting her off*) That's 30.

[MUSIC NO. 4A: TINA—PLAYOFF]

(*LIGHTS go out on TINA. Both WOMEN exit upstage R., with the chrome Videomatch chair. The panel flies out as . . .*)

* * *

LOUIS #1

LOUIS (MAN #2) enters downstage L. with a table and a chair. He turns on a tape recorder: MUSIC is heard from the machine. Then the tape speaks in carefully measured tones. It is a man's voice (MAN #3 live on an offstage mic.)

TAPE. Lesson 5. Dinner Conversation. Listen and repeat. (*Beep*) I was married for a short time. I'm sorry, I've never told anyone this before. (*LOUIS tries it timidly.*)

LOUIS. I was married for a short time. I'm sorry, I've never told anyone this before.

TAPE. (*Beep*) I never knew my father. I'm sorry, I've never told anyone this before.

LOUIS. I never knew my father. I'm sorry, I've never told anyone—

TAPE. (*Beep*) The doctor gave me six months. But I think he was just being nice. I'm sorry, I've never told anyone this before.

LOUIS. The doctor gave me six months. But I think he—

TAPE. (*Beep*) Ever since Marion died, I scream at the sight of a piano. I'm sorry, I've never told anyone this before.

LOUIS. (*trying to catch up*) Ever since Marion died, I—

TAPE. (*Beep*) So purdata esta luna di miele a Niagra Falls. Mi scusa, no so parlata quino uno.

(*LOUIS is utterly lost. The TAPE beeps. The LIGHTS fade on LOUIS as he rolls the table off downstage* L.)

* * *

A NIGHT ALONE

[MUSIC NO. 5]

A platform with a TV cart and SAM's chair rolls on from stage R. *as a door unit rolls on from stage* L. *SAM (MAN #1) enters from upstage* R. *and crosses to the upstage* L. *window. SAM is alone in his apartment.*

SAM.
A NIGHT ALONE.
AN EVENING FREE.
NO CLEVER PLANS,
NO PLACE TO BE,
A CHANCE TO COOL OUT AND COLLECT,
PERHAPS TO INTROSPECT,
OR MAYBE JUST GET TOTALLY WRECKED.
A NIGHT THAT'S ALL FOR ME.

I'M AWARE OF THE HUM
OF THE DIGITAL CLOCK
AND THE SOUND OF THE CAT
AS HE SLOWLY DESTROYS THE UPHOLSTERY.

SO I GO TO THE FRIDGE,
IS THERE SOMETHING TO EAT?
NO, THERE'S NOTHING BUT KODACHROME FILM
AND AN OLD JAR OF CHEESE SPREAD.

THEN I CURL UP TO READ,
BUT THE BOOK IS TOO THICK,
AND THE PAGE IS TOO THIN,
AND THE PRINT IS TOO SMALL,
AND IT'S ALL,
ABOUT MOSCOW!

(*He goes to his intercom and presses the buzzer.*)

MAN'S VOICE (MAN #2). Yeah?

SAM. Hi, Mario? It's Sam in 15-B.

VOICE. Yeah?

SAM. I was just wondering if there is any, uh, dry cleaning or packages or anything for me.

VOICE. No.

SAM. How are you?

VOICE. (*noncommittal*) I'm okay.

SAM. What's new down there?

VOICE. Well, it's just me and the door mostly. People come, people go . . .

SAM. How's your hip?

VOICE. Better. Look, Mr. Wagner, I've gotta go. People are coming. If you want, I could give you Eddie's number in the basement. He would talk to you.

SAM. No, no. That's okay. 'Night, Mario. (*SAM paces upstage as he sings.*)

SO I PACE AND I POKE
AND I SMOKE HALF A PACK
AS I PICK THE DEAD LEAVES
OFF MY FICAS THAT'S DYING OF ROOT ROT.

(*He crosses upstage and produces dead leaves. He then gets a scotch bottle from the T.V. cart and sits in the chair.*)

SO I HAUL OUT THE SCOTCH
AND FLIP ON THE TV,
BUT THE ONLY THING ON IS
A PROGRAM CALLED "EYE ON NEW JERSEY".

SO I'M ROLLING MY PENNIES
AND JUGGLING SOCKS
THEN IT'S BACK TO THE BOOK
AND THE FRIDGE AND THE CAT
AND THAT'S
WHEN I START HUNTING DUST BUNNIES!

(*He pulls out a large dust bunny from under the chair.*)

(*On his knees at the phone:*)
OH LORD,
MAKE THE PHONE RING.
MAKE IT SOMEBODY WONDERFUL.
YOU CAN DO IT, LORD.
IT'S NO BIG THING.
MAKE IT RING, LORD,
MAKE IT RING
MAKE IT RING
MAKE IT RING!
(*His doorbell buzzes.*)
(*Heavenward*) Close enough!

(*He opens the door. CLAIRE enters. There is an immediate attraction.*)

CLAIRE. Hi. I, uh, I live next door to you.

SAM. You do? What happened to the lady with the dog?

CLAIRE. I don't know. I've been living here for about a year. Haven't seen her yet.

SAM. Ah.

CLAIRE. Listen, I'm having a party tonight and I wondered if you had a blender I could borrow?

SAM. Sure, just a second. (*He exits and returns quickly with a large blender.*) Here. It only works on "whip". And you have to jiggle it a little. (*Introducing himself:*) Uh, Sam.

CLAIRE. Uh, Claire. Thanks. (*Pause.*) Listen, if you're free tonight maybe you'd like to join us?

SAM. I—

CLAIRE. (*kidding*) Come on, there'll be lots of people you don't know.

SAM. Well, that sounds like—

(*Suddenly, MAN #3 appears at the door with a casserole dish.*)

MAN #3. Claire, there you are. The doorman buzzed but there wasn't any answer. (*introducing himself to SAM*) Hi. I'm Tony Lambusco. I'm her date. Claire, I gotta put this in your fridge. My tuna mousse is melting.

CLAIRE. You go ahead. I'll be right in.

MAN #3. (*suspicious*) Yeah.

CLAIRE. (*after MAN #3 exits*) So, whadya say?

SAM. (*smiling*) No, thanks, I've got lots of things I've got to do tonight. Really. I have to . . . do things.

CLAIRE. Okay. Well, tell me if the music gets too loud. Thanks for the blender.

(*She exits. He sits. Long pause, then he sings.*)

SAM.
I'M AWARE OF THE HUM
OF THE DIGITAL CLOCK AND,
(*He looks at the clock.*)
OH MY GOD—
IT'S ONLY 8:30.

(*SAM exits stage* R. *with the platform. The LIGHTS fade and the door rolls off* L.)

* * *

[MUSIC NO. 5A: INTO RICKI BUSH]

VIDEOMATCH—RICKI

CLAIRE enters from stage R. *with the Videomatch chair and clipboard as the Videomatch panel flies in. LIGHTS come up on the Videomatch area. A rather unpleasant woman, RICKI BUSH (WOMAN #3) enters and slouches into the chair. CLAIRE watches her.*

CLAIRE. 30 seconds. Whatever you want.

(*The LIGHT comes on. RICKI looks at the camera.*)

RICKI BUSH. Look: I'm Ricki Bush. I don't want a loser. Some downer who's gonna drag me into the pits. I get enough of that in the rest of my life. I'm here to find a winner. But I don't want

any Peter Pan, either. Some guy way out in like Never Never
Land. And I don't need any mama's boys, alright? I'm not here
to be your mother. Oh, and I hate intellectual types or anyone
who's into cars or clothes. What do I need to let you into my life
for, huh? Look: I just don't want a guy who's a down, that's all.
I want somebody who's fun. Like me. (*She gets up and goes
toward the light.*)

You can shut that thing off 'cause that's all I gotta say.

(*CLAIRE signals for the camera to be turned off. RICKI exits
upstage L. The lights fade center as the Videomatch panel
flies out. CLAIRE exits with the chair upstage R.*)

[MUSIC NO. 5B: OUT OF RICKI BUSH]

* * *

LOUIS #2

*Lights come up on LOUIS as he rolls his table on downstage L.
He turns on the tape recorder. The recorded music is heard
again. The TAPE speaks.*

TAPE. (*MAN #3—live offstage*) Lesson 6. After Dinner
Strategy. Listen and respond. (*Beep*)

(*A woman's voice speaks, soft and romantic.*)

TAPE. (*WOMAN #3—live offstage*) Thank you. I had a
wonderful time.
LOUIS. (*summoning courage*) So . . . would you like to come
back to my apartment?
TAPE. So would you like to come back to my apartment?
LOUIS. (*caught off guard*) Uh, either one is fine.
TAPE. Or we can go to your apartment.
LOUIS. (*quick to agree*) Or we can go to my apartment.
TAPE. Whatever you say.
LOUIS. (*taking the initiative*) Okay, we'll go to my apartment.
TAPE. I think you'll like it, I just had it redecorated.
LOUIS. (*trying to keep up*) So we're going to your apartment.
TAPE. Or we can go someplace else.
LOUIS. No, your apartment's fine.

TAPE. We could see a movie.

LOUIS. Why?

TAPE. We could catch the midnight show.

LOUIS. (*It's slipping through his fingers.*) No!

TAPE. (*suddenly*) Wait a minute.

LOUIS. What?

TAPE. (*accusing*) What do you think you're doing?

LOUIS. (*has no idea*) I don't know. What am I doing?

TAPE. (*indignant*) What did you think I had in mind?

LOUIS. I'm sorry . . . you initially suggested—

TAPE. (*giggling suddenly*) Just kidding. We'll go to my apartment.

LOUIS. (*humorlessly*) Ha ha ha.

(*The LIGHTS fade on LOUIS as he exits with his table downstage L.*)

* * *

I THINK YOU SHOULD KNOW

[MUSIC NO. 6]

Platform moves on from stage R. with KIM's chair and telephone. Loveseat rolls on from stage L. with MAN #1. During the set change, KIM enters and sets her phone machine on. A voiceover is heard:

KIM'S VOICE. (*pre-recorded*) Hi. This is Kim. I can't come to the phone right now, but please leave a message after you hear the beep. Thanks.

(*LIGHTS up on KIM and MAN #1 in her apartment.*)

KIM.
I THINK YOU SHOULD KNOW
THIS IS MY FIRST TIME
SINCE I LEFT MICHAEL,
HE WAS MY HUSBAND.
I THINK YOU SHOULD KNOW
IN CASE I FAINT OR SCREAM OR DIE,
IN CASE I CALL OUT HIS NAME
YOU'LL UNDERSTAND WHY.

I THINK YOU SHOULD KNOW
IT'S NOT GOOD TO KISS ME THERE.
IT MAKES ME NAUSEOUS.
MY NECK'S VERY SENSITIVE.
BUT HOW COULD YOU KNOW?
WE ONLY MET THREE HOURS AGO.
OH, GOD, DO THAT AGAIN.
I-I-I THINK YOU SHOULD KNOW:

I'VE BEEN DREAMING OF THIS MOMENT
FOR SUCH A LONG TIME.
I WISH I'D CLEANED MY APARTMENT.
YOU HAVE VERY NICE SKIN.
I'VE BEEN WAITING FOR THIS MOMENT
FOR SUCH A LONG TIME.
YOU ARE MY FANTASY.
BUT BEFORE WE BEGIN:

I THINK YOU SHOULD KNOW
THAT YOU'RE THE ONLY ONE,
OTHER THAN MICHAEL,
HE WAS MY HUSBAND.
AND YOU SHOULD KNOW
YES — NO —
I THINK THE WINE WENT TO MY HEAD.
I'LL GO MAKE US A SNACK.
OH, WAIT! DON'T FOLD OUT THE BED.

I THINK YOU SHOULD KNOW
I DROPPED OUT OF COLLEGE.
I THINK YOU SHOULD KNOW
I DON'T SPEAK WITH MY MOTHER.
I THINK YOU SHOULD KNOW
I TALK WHEN I'M NERVOUS.
I LOVE WHEN YOU TOUCH ME.
I LOVE HAROLD ROBBINS.
I THINK I SHOULD KNOW
ALOT MORE ABOUT YOU THAN I DO.

I THINK YOU SHOULD KNOW
I THINK YOU SHOULD KNOW
THAT I THINK YOU SHOULD . . . GO . . .
I THINK.

(*The LIGHTS fade as the stage clears.*)

* * *

TYPESETTER #3

*LIGHTS come up on the TYPESETTER seated on a lawn chair
    downstage* L. *He is going through a large billfold of
    photographs.*

TYPESETTER. (*beaming*) What a vacation! (*He holds out pictures for the audience to see.*)
    This is the three of us in front of the Magic Castle. (*shows
another picture*)
    And here's Adelle and Blini and Dopey. (*another picture*)
    This is just Blini in front of "It's a Small World After All".
(*final shot*)
    This is just me and Blini in front of the hotel. (*He sets the pic-
tures down.*)
    Boy, it was just what he needed. He's been like a new person
ever since we got back. Laughing to himself all the time. And
singing. And, well, then, last night Adelle and I were in bed.
And all of a sudden she whispers, "Why don't we invite in Mr.
Blini?" Now I was a little surprised. This coming from a woman
who, as far as I know, has never even seen herself naked. So I
think she's kidding. The next thing I know, he's standing in the
door carrying three glasses and a bottle of Cold Duck. Adelle
slaps on the Tony Bennet and, uh, what can I tell you . . . that
little guy's terriffic.

(*LIGHTS fade on the TYPESETTER, as his chair rolls off* L.)

* * *

[MUSIC NO. 6A: HANNAH KLEINE NEXTMUSIK]

VIDEOMATCH—HANNAH

The Videomatch panel flies in. CLAIRE enters stage R. *with
    chair, followed by HANNAH (WOMAN #3). HANNAH
    sits in the chair. The LIGHT goes on.*

HANNAH. Hi. My name is Hannah Klein. Well, you should

know right off the bat that I'm kind of open to anything. Specifically, I'm either looking for a woman who is not afraid to be caretaking or for a man who is willing to be vulnerable. However, I think you should know, if you're the woman, I'll probably try to turn you into my mother, at which point I'll begin to resent you and secretly wish I were involved with a man. On the other hand, for you men, I'll probably feel a tremendous amount of anger towards you, which may or may not have to do with my father, and begin to seek out deeper relationships with my women friends. The really difficult part starts for either men or women when I force you to reject me, which in turn alienates you and causes both of us to act out destructive patterns that were established long before we ever met. If this sounds good to you, and you like skiing, Beethoven and quiet nights by the fire, then maybe I'm the woman for you. Or you.

CLAIRE. That's thirty, Dr. Klein.

(*The LIGHTS fade. HANNAH and CLAIRE exit upstage R. with the Videomatch chair as the panel flies out.*)

* * *

SECOND GRADE

[MUSIC NO. 7]

LIGHTS come up on a bare stage. MAN #1 and MAN #2 stand downstage R. holding beer mugs. They are telling jokes. MAN #3 enters and crosses to them.

MAN #1. There he is!
MAN #2. Hey hey! Hey hey hey!
MAN #3. How ya doin'?

(*There is a warm back-slapping, arm-punching greeting.*)

MAN #1. Look at him, wearing a suit. Well here we are.
MAN #3. Together again.

(*Pause.*)

MAN #2. (*like an old game they used to play*) Alright, okay, alright, okay, alright, okay, alright . . . Okay! So who's married?

Man #1. Not me.

Man #3. Not me.

Man #2. Not me. Anymore.

All. Alright, okay!!!!

Man #3. A toast: (*MUSIC begins.*)

THOSE WERE THE DAYS,

Man #1.

YEAH, THOSE WERE THE DAYS,

Man #2.

GETTIN' INTO TROUBLE FOR THE HELL WE'D RAISE.

(*MEN pass beer mugs offstage.*)

Man #3.

REMEMBER WHEN . . .

Man #1.

IT WAS BETTER THEN . . .

All.

OH, I WISH WE COULD GO BACK AGAIN

TO SECOND GRADE,
AH, SECOND GRADE,
THE MEMORY WILL NEVER FADE,
WHEN GIRLS WERE GIRLS AND MEN WERE BOYS,
AND NO ONE MADE YOU SHARE YOUR TOYS.
OH, WE HAD IT MADE
IN SECOND GRADE.

(*LIGHTS shift and MAN #1 moves to WOMAN #3 who has entered and is sitting on a washing machine stage R. reading a book.*)

Man #1. It's great since they put in all the new dryers, huh? (*She smiles politely and returns to her book.*) Can I get you a soda from the machine? Some gum? Little box of Tide? (*She doesn't even smile. In reply, she holds up an economy size bottle of "Solo" detergent. He indicates the book.*) What, do you have a test on that thing tomorrow? (*She sighs and moves farther away.*) Listen, I'm a nice guy. Really. Think we could just talk for a while? Like maybe until the rinse cycle? (*She continues to ignore him.*) Hello? Alright . . . (*He is suddenly eight years old. He grabs the book from her hand.*) Nya, Nya, Nya, Nya, Nya, Nya, Nya!

Woman #3. Give it to me.

MAN #1. Okay. (*He pulls her hair, gives her several noogies on her shoulder then twists the skin on her arm.*) Indian burn!!

(*He laughs and runs away. She screams. The washing machine and WOMAN #3 move offstage L. as a platform with a restaurant table, 2 chairs and WOMAN #1 appears stage R. and moves center. MAN #3 sits with WOMAN #1 at the table.*)

WOMAN #1. I feel like you don't know what you want. I keep getting mixed signals from you. (*He appears uncomfortable and says nothing.*)
You say you love me and then I don't hear from you for a week. You say you see a future in our relationship but you are not willing to discuss it. What am I supposed to think? (*He is at a loss.*) Say something, Richard.

MAN #3. (*mimicking her like a little brother*) "Say something, Richard."

WOMAN #1. This is our relationship I'm talking about.

MAN #3. (*mimicking*) "This is our relationship I'm talking about."

WOMAN #1. (*exasperated*) Waiter, can we have the check, please?

MAN #3. (*again, mimicking*) "Waiter, can we have the check, please?"

(*The platform rolls offstage R. with WOMAN #1. The three MEN come together and sing.*)

MEN.
THOSE WERE THE DAYS,
YEAH, THOSE WERE THE DAYS.
   MAN #3.
EIGHT CRAYOLA COLORS—
AND NONE OF THEM WERE GRAYS.
   ALL.
REMEMBER WHEN . . .
   MAN #3.
IT WAS BETTER THEN . . .
   ALL.
OH I WISH WE COULD GO BACK AGAIN TO

MISS MALONE,
AH, MISS MALONE,
THE ONLY REAL WOMAN WE'VE EVER KNOWN,
SHE'D CLIP YOUR MITTENS AND ZIP YOUR HOOD,
MAN #2.
YOU GOT A GOLD STAR SO YOU KNEW WHERE YOU
STOOD.
WHERE ARE YOU NOW THAT WE'VE GROWN,
MISS MALONE?

(*The lights shift and MAN #2 crosses to WOMAN #2 who stands holding two suitcases.*)

WOMAN #2. I'll be by for the rest of my stuff next week. If you need me for anything I left Paul's number by the fridge.
MAN #2. Okay.
WOMAN #2. We're doing the right thing.
MAN #2. Sure.
WOMAN #2. Do you think, if we give it some time, after a while we can be friends?
MAN #2. I hope so.
WOMAN #2. (*puts out her hand to shake his goodbye*) Bye, bye.
MAN #2. (*reaches into his pocket, pulls out a water gun and squirts her in the face*) Bang! Bang! Bang! Bang! (*She runs out. He blows the smoke from the end of his gun.*)
Got her!

(*The three MEN sing.*)

MAN #3.
REMEMBER WHEN WE WERE EIGHT,
MAN #1.
WE SURE THOUGHT THIRTY-FOUR WOULD BE GREAT:
MAN #2.
NO ONE HOLDING OUR HAND, TELLING US WHAT TO
DO,
ALL.
AND SON OF A BITCH, IT ALL CAME TRUE!
OH, GOD, I WISH WE'D STAYED,
OH, WE HAD IT MADE,
MAN #1.
I'D EVEN GIVE UP GETTING LAID

(*MAN #2 calls MAN #1 over and slaps him in the face.*)

ALL.
TO BE BACK IN SECOND GRADE!

(*The MEN exit.*)

* * *

[MUSIC NO. 7A: GRADE B PLAYOFF]

LOUIS #3

LIGHTS up on LOUIS' table downstage L. He enters and turns the tape on. We hear the MUSIC and then the TAPE speaks.

TAPE. (MAN #3). Lesson 10. Listen and respond. (*Beep*)

TAPE. (WOMAN #3). (*in the throes of passion*) Oh yes. Oh god that's good. Yes. Talk dirty. Talk dirty to me.

LOUIS. Uh . . .

TAPE. Come on!

LOUIS. Uh . . . uh . . . nipples!

TAPE. Oh yes! Now a little lower.

LOUIS. (*uncertain, in a deep voice and bending his knees*) Nipples.

TAPE. Yes! Oh, don't stop. Don't. Don't stop. Don't sto— Why did you stop? Why did you stop? (*Beep*)

(*LOUIS is panicked. He has no answer. Rather than deal with the question, he fast forwards the tape to a later lesson.*)

TAPE. (MAN #3) Lesson 13.

TAPE. (WOMAN #3). (*in the afterglow*) This isn't a one night thing for you, is it? That would really upset me. This better not be a one night thing.

LOUIS. (*trying*) Uh, no. It's not. No it's not.

TAPE. (*putting him on the spot*) Then what is it? (*Beep*)

(*LOUIS doesn't have any idea what to say, so he again fast forwards it to a later lesson.*)

TAPE (MAN #3). Lesson 17.

Tape (Woman #3). (*enthusiastically*) You know what we're going to do? We're going to drop all our defenses. Let down the walls. We're going to "feel" things. We're going to make ourselves more vulnerable than we've ever been before. Ready . . . Set . . .

(*Before she can say "go", LOUIS speeds away. Fast forward.*)

Tape (Man #3). Lesson 31.
Tape (Woman #3). (*upset and angry*) Don't give me that! You can't be laughing *with* me, because I'm not laughing!!!

(*Fast forward.*)

Tape (Man #3). Lesson 34.
Tape (Woman #3). (*suddenly seductive*) Come here. Come on. Come here. (*LOUIS hesitates at the fast forward button.*) I'm sorry I haven't been myself lately.
Louis. (*running his finger along the tape recorder*) That's okay.
Tape (Woman #3). Mmmmm. That's nice.
Louis. Yeah?
Tape (Woman #3). I've missed you.
Louis. You have?
Tape (Man #3). (*deep man's voice*) I've missed you too.
Louis. Hey, who are you?
Tape (Man #3). Who are you?
Louis. I'm . . . I'm Louis.
Tape (Woman #3). He's the one I was telling you about.
Tape (Man #3). Want me to hit him?
Louis. No!
Tape (Woman #3). No. Yeah, hit him.
Louis. NO!

(*He quickly fast forwards.*)

Tape (Man #3). Lesson 40.
Tape (Woman #3). (*She is crying now.*) Where are we? I don't know where we are anymore. (*Beep*) I don't know who you are anymore. (*LOUIS sits.*) (*Beep*) I don't know where we're going. Where are we going? (*Beep*) Why am I crying? (*Beep*) Who are we kidding? And why won't you let me make you happy!?!

(*Sound of a door slamming and feet going down a hall.*)

TAPE (MAN #3). You have now reached the end of the first cycle. Uh-oh. You're single again. So what do you do?

LOUIS. (*destroyed*) I don't know. What do I do?

TAPE (MAN #3). Right. You flip the tape and move on to the second cycle.

(*LOUIS obediently flips the cassette. Recorded MUSIC.*)

TAPE (MAN #3). Cycle 2. Pursuing the Unattainable. Married Women, Lesbians and Women of the Clergy. (*Beep*)

(*LIGHTS fade on LOUIS.*)

* * *

IMAGINE MY SURPRISE

[MUSIC NO. 8]

CLAIRE enters, as the Videomatch panel flies in. The set is now the back of the Videomatch studio. CLAIRE speaks to an unseen client upstage of the panel:

CLAIRE. Hi. 30 seconds when the light comes on. (*She cues the camera, turns around and sings:*)
I NEVER BELIEVED
THAT I'D MEET A MAN
WITH WHOM I COULD SPEND
THE REST OF MY LIFE.
I NEVER BELIEVED
IN SOME CHARMING PRINCE
OR A MAN OF MY DREAMS.
AND SINCE
I NEVER BELIEVED
THAT ANY OF THAT CRAP WAS TRUE,
IMAGINE MY SURPRISE
WHEN I MET YOU.

I MET YOU
AND IT'S TRUMPETS AND BELLS

AND IT'S BIRDS
AND IT'S WORDS
LIKE "RAPTURE" AND "JOY",
AND BOY, I COULDN'T BELIEVE IT.

BUT I ALWAYS BELIEVED
THAT SOONER OR LATER
YOU'D SOMEHOW SLIP UP
AND SAY SOMETHING DUMB.
SOME THOUGHTLESS REMARK,
BUT I'D SUDDENLY PAUSE
AND YOU'D BE NOTHING SPECIAL.
BECAUSE
I ALWAYS BELIEVED
THAT NO ONE COULD STAY SO GOOD,
IMAGINE MY SURPRISE
WHEN YOU COULD.

AND YOU DID.
AND GOT BETTER AND BETTER,
WHILE I JUST STOOD BY
FALLING DEEPER, AND THEN,
AGAIN, I COULDN'T BELIEVE IT,
BUT I WOKE UP ONE DAY
AND SAW MY DEFENSES,
MY WELL THOUGHT OUT
CAREFULLY CHOSEN DEFENSES,
MY IRON CLAD,
HARD-BOILED,
INSOLUBLE WALLS
HAD LAYER
BY LAYER
BY LAYER
BEEN MELTED AWAY.

AND I STILL CAN'T BELIEVE
I MET A MAN
WITH WHOM I COULD SPEND
THE REST OF MY LIFE.
I STILL CAN'T BELIEVE
THAT YOU'RE REALLY GONE,
THAT THE MAN OF MY DREAMS
IS GONE.

I STILL CAN'T BELIEVE
THAT IT NEVER OCCURRED TO ME
I MIGHT NOT BE THE DREAM FOR YOU.
IMAGINE MY SURPRISE.

(*LIGHTS fade on CLAIRE. Blackout.*)

* * *

I'D RATHER DANCE ALONE

[MUSIC NO. 9]

LIGHTS up on the COMPANY on a bare stage, dancing with mannequins.

MAN #2.
HER DRESS IS KAMALI.
HER MAKE-UP'S KABUKI.
SORT OF SALVADORE DALI
MEETS YOUNG PAT SUZUKI.
I'M OUT ON A DATE IN THE TWILIGHT ZONE.
I'D RATHER DANCE ALONE.

WOMAN #3.
I'M INTELLECTUAL
HE'S INTO LEATHER.
I WOKE UP TODAY
WITH MY HANDS TIED TOGETHER.
AND THERE'S THIS THING THAT HE DOES WITH THE
   CORD TO THE PHONE!
I'D RATHER DANCE ALONE.
   MAN #1.
SHE'S INTO CROSS-DRESSING.
   WOMAN #2.
HIS TOUPEE IS SHEDDING.
   MAN #3.
OUR SEX LIFE'S DEPRESSING.
   WOMAN #1.
HE'S PLANNING THE WEDDING.
   ALL.
YOU PASS THROUGH MY LIFE LIKE A KIDNEY STONE!
I'D RATHER DANCE ALONE!

I'D RATHER
HOLD OUT,
I'M NOT GONNA SETTLE,
HOLD OUT,
IT'S NEVER TOO LATE.
HOLD OUT,
I KNOW WHAT I WANT
AND I'M WILLING TO WAIT.

HOLD OUT,
I'D RATHER DANCE—
HOLD OUT,
DANCE, DANCE, DANCE!
HOLD OUT,
I'D RATHER DANCE ALONE!!

(*They dispose of their dummies and dance.*)

I'D RATHER
HOLD OUT,
I'M NOT GONNA SETTLE,
HOLD OUT,
IT'S NEVER TOO—

(*They suddenly pause, seeing someone incredibly desirable
    across the room.*)

I'VE GOTTA BE DREAMING.
  WOMEN.
HE'S APOLLO IN PANTS.
  MEN.
SHE'S PRACTICALLY STEAMING.
  ALL.
I SHOULD ASK HIM/HER TO DANCE.
AND DO I STAND A CHANCE
NEXT TO ALL THE INCREDIBLE LOVERS HE'S/SHE'S
    PROBABLY KNOWN?
I'D RATHER DANCE ALONE.

I'D RATHER
HOLD OUT,
I'M NOT GONNA SETTLE,

HOLD OUT,
IT'S NEVER TOO LATE.
I'M GONNA HOLD OUT,
I KNOW WHAT I WANT
AND I'M WILLING TO WAIT.

HOLD OUT,
I'D RATHER DANCE—
HOLD OUT,
DANCE, DANCE, DANCE!
HOLD OUT,
FUCK ROMANCE!
HOLD OUT,
I'D RATHER DANCE ALONE!!
ALONE!!
ALONE!!

(*Blackout. The show drop flies in. A spotlight picks out an ad:*)

Boop: Come back—C.B.

END ACT ONE

ACT TWO

MOVING IN WITH LINDA

[MUSIC NO. 10]

Through a door upstage, TWO MOVERS (MAN #2 and MAN #3) bring on a very big box. They exit. SAM (MAN #1) enters holding another box. He is alone onstage, in an empty apartment. MUSIC.

SAM. (*sings*)
I'M MOVING IN WITH LINDA!
IT'S A BIG STEP,
BUT I CAN'T WAIT,
IT'S A FRESH START,
IT'S A CLEAN SLATE,
FOUR WHITE WALLS
AND LINDA
AND ME.

(*The TWO MOVERS enter with baggage: trunks and boxes.*)

MOVER. Where d'ya want it?

(*SAM indicates a spot. As the MOVERS exit, he opens the box and removes contents.*)

SAM.
THIS CASSEROLE WILL BE *OUR* CASSEROLE,
THIS CROCKPOT WILL COOK *OUR* STEW.
EVEN THESE LITTLE BAGGIE TWIST 'EMS WILL BE
  OUR BAGGIE TWIST 'EMS,
FOR THE LEFTOVERS LEFT OVER FROM A DINNER
  FOR TWO. OOH.

(*The MOVERS re-enter with more stuff, including a garment bag. SAM sings to them.*)

SAM.	MOVERS.
I'M MOVING IN WITH LINDA!	HE'S MOVING IN WITH LINDA
IT'S A BIT SMALL	OOOOOOOH.

46

BUT NO COMPLAINT,   (*The MOVERS exit.*)
TAKE A DEEP BREATH
JUST SMELL THAT PAINT.
IT'S THREE AND A HALF ROOMS
AND LINDA
AND ME.
AND ME.

(*ELAINE [WOMAN #2] appears out of the garment bag.*)

ELAINE. (*singing from the open bag*)
AND ME!
(*She steps out of the bag.*)
SAM. Elaine! What are you doing here? We broke up eight years ago. You're living in San Francisco.
ELAINE. Where should I put this?
SAM. What is it?
ELAINE. It's the plaster bust of Cervantes that we got at the Plaza de Toros the day we swam naked in the fountain and swore we'd spend the rest of our lives together.
SAM. Ah.
ELAINE. (*sings*)
REMEMBER SPAIN, SAM?
THE NIGHT THAT WE SPENT
ON THAT TRAIN TO MADRID,
GETTING SMASHED ON CHEAP ROJO
AND OJO, THE THINGS THAT WE DID.
SAM. Yeah.
ELAINE.
WE MADE LOVE TO THE RHYTHM OF WHEELS
AND RATTLING GLASS.
SAM.
THE COMPARTMENT WAS TOURIST,
BUT WE WERE FIRST CLASS.
BOTH.
THAT NIGHT ON THE TRAIN,
ELAINE.
SAM
BOTH.
WE PROMISED EACH OTHER A LIFETIME OF SPAIN,
ELAINE.
SAM.

SAM.
OH ELAINE!
ELAINE. (*stopping him*)
SAM—
YOU'RE MOVING IN WITH LINDA.
SAM. Right. Right.
ELAINE.
IT'S A BOLD MOVE,
CAN'T TURN BACK.
SAM.
AND IT'S WHAT I WANT.
ELAINE.
SO UNPACK.
SAM.
FROM HERE ON IN
IT'S LINDA,
MOVER. (*entering with more baggage*) Where d'ya want it?
SAM.
OOH MY SWEET, SWEET LINDA,
AND ME.

(*MARILOU [WOMAN #1] pops out of the big box.*)

MARILOU. AND ME!
SAM. Marilou Huntzinger?

(*She is dressed in a cheerleader's outfit and carries pom-poms.*)

MARILOU.
Action! Action! We want action!
A-C-T . . . I-O-N!
Go, Panthers!!!
SAM. (*to MARILOU*) Hi. (*ELAINE clears her throat. SAM is stunned.*) Uh, Elaine, this is Marilou. Marilou, Elaine.
MARILOU. Hi.
ELAINE. Hi.
SAM. (*to ELAINE*) Marilou was the Homecoming Queen from my high school. She was also my lab partner in Biology 2. She didn't know I was alive. I'm really surprised she's here.
MARILOU. (*singing*)
I WANTED YOU, STAN.
SAM. (*correcting her*) Sam.

MARILOU.
—SAM.
AS YOUR STRONG STEADY HAND
PINNED THAT FROG TO THE CORK,
YOU WERE NOT YET A MAN,
YET SOMEHOW NO LONGER A DORK.
  SAM. Yeah?
  MARILOU.
AH, THE THRILL WE DISCOVERED
UNCOVERING ORGANS UNKNOWN,
I CAN STILL SMELL FORMALDEHYDE
MIXED WITH YOUR JADE EAST COLOGNE.
AND YOU NEVER KNEW, SAM
THAT I LEFT MY HEART IN BIOLOGY TWO, SAM.
  SAM.
MARILOU!
  MARILOU.
SAM—
  ELAINE.
REMEMBER SPAIN, SAM!
  SAM.
OH ELAINE!
  MARILOU.
SAM
  BOTH WOMEN.
I WANT YOU!
  SAM.
WHAT TO DO?

(*The MOVERS re-enter pushing a large trunk.*)

  MOVERS.
COMIN' THROUGH!
  SAM. No! Wait! Wait a minute, wait a minute! I don't want
this. It's not mine.
  ELAINE. It's got your name on it. (*He looks down at it. The
words "Sam's Trunk" are boldly emblazoned on the front.*)
  MOVER. (*setting down trunk*) Buddy, come on, I got a whole
truckload of this stuff.
  SAM. (*horrified*) You do?!
  MOVER. Yeah, buddy, you got more baggage than any guy I
ever seen.

(*The MOVERS laugh, and they exit. The trunk lid begins to open.*)

SAM. (*sitting on lid*) No! Back! (*to himself:*) Oh God, wake up. (*to trunk:*) Go away! I'm not letting you out! I don't care who you are!

(*We hear the voice of RENE [WOMAN #3] from inside the trunk.*)

RENE. (*coolly*) It's Rene.

SAM. Oh shit. (*to the others*) How do I look? (*He opens the trunk. She emerges.*) Hello, Rene. I haven't seen you since you threw that plate of Veal Picatta at my head at Tavern on the Green. How've you been?

RENE. (*sings*)
SO YOU'RE MOVING IN WITH LINDA?
WELL, YOU'RE A BIG BOY,
IT'S YOUR OWN LIFE.
WHAT DO I KNOW,
I WAS ALMOST HIS WIFE.

SAM. (*spoken*)
I WAS GONNA TELL YOU
(*sung*)
ABOUT LINDA
AND—

RENE.
THIS CASSEROLE WAS ONCE *OUR* CASSEROLE,
THIS CROCKPOT ONCE COOKED *OUR* STEW.

SAM. You're not bitter about this, are you?

RENE.
I ALWAYS WONDERED WHAT HAPPENED TO THESE
    LITTLE BAGGIE TWIST 'EMS
THEY COULD HAVE HELD MY HEART TOGETHER
WHEN YOU SAID WE WERE THROUGH!

SAM. Oh God, take them.

RENE. No, no. No, no, no. They're part of your new life now. Your new life with Linda.

WOMEN. (*sing*)
SAM AND LINDA
SAM AND LINDA
BONG BONG BONG BONG

ONLY LINDA
ALWAYS LINDA
  ELAINE.
ONLY LINDA
  MARILOU, RENE.
BONG BONG BONG BONG
  MARILOU.
FOREVER AND EVER LINDA
  WOMEN.
DAYS AND NIGHTS
AND NIGHTS AND DAYS
AND DAYS AND NIGHTS OF LINDA
  RENE.
AN ETERNITY OF LINDA.
  WOMEN.
BONG BONG BONG BONG
BONG BONG BONG BONG . . .
  SAM. (*overlapping*) You don't scare me.
I'VE CHANGED!
I'VE GROWN!
I'M READY FOR A COMMITMENT
I'M READY FOR

(*The MOVERS enter with phone handset.*)

  WOMEN & MOVER #2. (*Operatic high note:*)
THE PHONE!

(*He produces the phone. SAM shoots him a look and answers
  it.*)

SAM.	WOMEN. (*while SAM is*
Hello?	*on the phone*)
VOICE.	BONG BONG BONG BONG
(*taped offstage*)	HE'S NOT READY
Hi Sam. It's Didi.	BONG BONG BONG BONG
SAM. Didi?	HE'S NOT READY
VOICE. Didi, from Tuesday	
night. Listen, did I leave a tube	
or Orthogynol cream in the	
right hand pocket of your	
sports jacket?	

(*SAM puts his hand in his
　　pocket. He freezes.*)

Sam. Listen, Didi, I can't talk
to you right now.

(*SAM hangs up. The MOVERS exit with the phone.*)

Women. (*seducing him*)
HE'S NOT READY
READY TO MAKE A COMMITMENT
HE'LL NEVER BE READY
NO, NO, NO . . .

(*SAM ad libs during this.*)

Women.
HE'S NOT READY
NO, NO, NO . . .
NO, NO, NO . . .
NO, NO—

(*There is a knock at the door. They all freeze.*)

Sam. Go away. I can't take anymore.
Voice. (*taped offstage*) Honey, it's me.
Sam. Linda! Just a second, sweetheart. There's some stuff
blocking the door.

(*He frantically begins to stuff the three WOMEN back in the
　　baggage. He sings quickly.*)

All.
I'M/HE'S MOVING IN WITH LINDA
IT'S A BIG STEP
BUT I/HE CAN'T WAIT.
IT'S A FRESH START
IT'S A CLEAN SLATE.
IT'S FOUR WHITE WALLS
AND . . .
　　Sam. (*pushing ELAINE'S head down*) Get back!!

RENE.
FOREVER AND EVER—
(*pushing her down*) Get back!!
MARILOU.
DAYS AND NIGHTS OF—
SAM. (*pushing her down*) Get back!!
FROM HERE ON IN
IT'S LINDA—

ELAINE.
AND ME.

MARILOU.
AND ME.

RENE.
AND ME.

(*They disappear. SAM opens the door and looks toward LINDA who remains unseen offstage.*)

SAM. Linda! Sweetheart! (*Beat. He looks beyond her. Uneasily:*) Are all those bags yours?

(*Blackout. The stage is cleared.*)

* * *

[MUSIC NO. 10A: LINDA—PLAYOFF]

A LITTLE HAPPINESS

LIGHTS come up on the TYPESETTER as his platform rolls on from stage R. He holds a tin of cookies and takes a bite of one.

TYPESETTER. You gotta try one of these. (*He offers a cookie to someone in the audience.*) You've never tasted cookies like this. He makes them. They've got all this stuff inside, like raisins and chocolate chips and coconut and some kind of nuts . . . (*MUSIC begins.*) [MUSIC NO. 11] Every bite is a surprise. (*He sings.*)

A LITTLE HAPPINESS

SO I'M FORTY-FIVE.
SO I THOUGHT MY LIFE WOULD ALWAYS BE
THE WAY IT'S ALWAYS BEEN,
THEN HE WALKED IN:
A LITTLE HAPPINESS.

SO NEIGHBORS THINK IT'S STRANGE
WHEN THEY SEE ADELLE AND ME AND BLI-
NI HAND IN HAND IN HAND.
THEY DON'T UNDERSTAND
A LITTLE HAPPINESS,

A LITTLE JOY.
SO PEOPLE STOP US ON THE STREET WITH
"WHAT AN UGLY LITTLE BOY".
IS THAT SUCH A PRICE TO PAY?
OKAY,

SO IT'S A LITTLE WEIRD,
SO MY WIFE AND I HAVE FALLEN FOR
THIS GUY WHO'S THREE-FOOT-TWO.
WELL SO WOULD YOU.
YOU'D BE SURPRISED
THE THINGS YOU DO
FOR A LITTLE HAPPINESS.

(*The LIGHTS fade as the TYPESETTER's platform rolls off* R.)

* * *

KIM'S MONOLOGUE

A platform with a female mannequin rolls on downstage L. *as a bus stop sign swings into position. KIM enters the bus stop. She recognizes an acquaintance (the mannequin). The mannequin is very pregnant.*

KIM. Oh, hi! How are you?! You look really . . . pregnant. I didn't even hear you got married. (*Pause as she listens to the mannequin.*) Unh huh. Congratulations. That's wonderful.

(*Pause.*) Uh, no, Michael and I, uh, split up—(*Pause.*) Yeah, well, I look at it this way: at least now I have something in common with my parents. (*Pause, uncomfortable laugh. She changes the subject.*)

So when are you due? (*Pause.*) Can I? (*She puts her hand on the mannequin's stomach. After a moment, she draws it away quickly.*)

Babies. Wow. (*There is a long pause as KIM looks wistfully at the woman's stomach.*)

Shouldn't you be home, like, near a phone? (*Pause.*) Oh. You're working? (*Pause.*) Senior Vice President of the whole company? (*Pause.*) Huh. So, I guess you're not still writing. (*Pause.*) You *are* still writing. (*Pause.*) What do you do on weekends? (*Pause.*) Well, I'm sure the blind children appreciate that. (*She looks off.*)

I, uh, I've got to go. Give Russ my love and congratulations on the job and the novel and the baby. (*Pause.*) I can't, that's my bus. I've gotta go throw myself under it.

[MUSIC NO. 11A: KIM'S PLAYOFF]

(*The LIGHTS fade as KIM exits downstage L. The platform rolls off after her.*)

* * *

I COULD ALWAYS GO TO YOU

[MUSIC NO. 12]

WOMAN #1 and WOMAN #3 enter with rolling stools, sit center stage, and sing.

BOTH.
LA LA LA LA—LA LA LA LA
LA LA LA LA—LA LA LA LA
LA LA LA LA—LA LA LA LA
LA LA LA
LA LA LA
MEN HAVE MOVED IN AND OUT OF OUR LIVES:
WOMAN #1.
SOME MAKING A MARK,

WOMAN #3.
SOME MAKING A MESS,
   WOMAN #1.
SOME GIVING MORE—
   WOMAN #3.
MORE GIVING LESS.
   WOMAN #1.
ONE BREAKING A HEART—
   WOMAN #3.
ONE TAKING A DRESS.
   WOMAN #1. (*Spoken*) Who?
   WOMAN #3. Tony. When I lived in Boston.
   WOMAN #1. Oh, right.
   BOTH.
BUT EVERY TIME I'D LAND ON MY ASS
WHO WAS THERE WITH A BOTTLE AND A GLASS?
AND NO MATTER WHAT WE WENT THROUGH
I KNEW I COULD ALWAYS GO TO YOU.

LA LA—LA LA LA LA
LA LA LA LA—LA LA LA LA
LA LA LA LA—LA LA LA LA
LA LA LA
LA LA LA
IT ALWAYS ENDS PRETTY MUCH THE SAME WAY:
   WOMAN #3.
EITHER BOB GETTING NEEDY
AND ME GETTING BORED.
   WOMAN #1.
OR JIMMY RESENTFUL
AND FEELING IGNORED.
   BOTH.
AND THE EXIT LINE
OF THE YEAR AWARD . . .
   WOMAN #3. (*Spoken*) . . . goes to Marcus who said, "If you really wanted this relationship, Patty, you wouldn't have gained those twenty two pounds."
   BOTH.
AND WHO WAS THERE WITH A SHOULDER AND A
   SMOKE?
WHO SAID, "FUCK 'EM IF THEY CAN'T TAKE A JOKE?"
AND NO MATTER WHAT WE WENT THROUGH
I KNEW I COULD ALWAYS GO TO YOU.

WOMAN #1.
AND WHEN I BROKE UP WITH BRAD
FOR THE SECOND –
(*WOMAN #3 indicates "three."*)
THIRD TIME,
WOMAN #3.
AND WHEN DR. BERNIE WRIGHT
TURNED INTO MR. BERNIE WRONG,
BOTH.
WE LOOKED AT EACH OTHER
AND SUDDENLY SAW
WHAT WE'D MISSED ALL ALONG:
WHO'S SEEN ME AT MY WORST?
WOMAN #1.
WHO SAW ME THROUGH MY FIRST?
BOTH.
WHO CAN I BE MYSELF AROUND,
UNINVITED, UNREHEARSED?
AND WITH ONE EMPHATIC, ECSTATIC, DRAMATIC
DECISION
WE KNEW ALL OUR PROBLEMS WERE SOLVED:
WE BECAME ROMANTICALLY INVOLVED.

LA LA – LA LA LA LA
LA LA LA LA – LA LA LA LA
LA LA LA LA – LA LA LA LA
LA LA LA
LA LA LA

THEN WE MOVED IN TOGETHER AND IN NO TIME AT
ALL,
WOMAN #1.
I BECAME NEEDY
AND YOU BECAME BORED,
WOMAN #3.
AND I WAS RESENTFUL
AND YOU FELT IGNORED.
BOTH.
AND THE EXIT LINE
OF THE YEAR AWARD . . .
WOMAN #1. (*spoken*) . . . goes to Patty, who said, "It's not the
salmon croquettes it's the whole goddam relationship!"
AND WHO LOCKED WHO OUT

WOMAN #3.
AND WHO CALLED WHO FAT?
  BOTH.
AND WHO COULD BELIEVE IT WOULD TURN INTO
  THAT?
AND THE WORST PART OF WHAT WE WENT THROUGH
WAS I KNEW I COULDN'T EVEN GO TO YOU.
LA LA LA
  WOMAN #3.
NOW I'M BACK WITH DR. BERNIE
  WOMAN #1.
AND I'M BACK BREAKING UP WITH BRAD.
  BOTH.
AND IT'S HARD TO SAY IF THIS IS BETTER
OR WORSE THAN WHAT WE HAD.
BUT IF WHAT APPEARS TO BE TRUE IS TRUE
AND BULLSHIT IS BULLSHIT
NO MATTER WHO—
THEN THIS IS WHAT I'D RATHER DO:
I'LL LIVE WITH THEM
AND HAVE LUNCH WITH YOU!

LA LA—LA LA LA LA
LA LA LA LA—LA LA LA LA
LA LA LA LA—LA LA LA LA
LA LA LA
LA LA

(*Both WOMEN exit upstage* R. *with stools. LIGHTS crossfade
  as . . .*)

* * *

GROUP

[MUSIC NO. 12A]

A large armchair rolls on from stage L.

VOICE-OVER. (*MAN #2 on tape, as the scene shifts.*) "Tired of
a simple one on one? Intimate group looking for new members.
Seeks hot couples/singles for daytime/nitetime pleasures.
Several positions available."

(*BOB [MAN #2] enters. He carries a top coat and briefcase. He looks about, then calls offstage:*)

BOB. Honeybears, I'm home.

(*From offstage, six voices respond in unison:*)

GROUP. Hi, Pudding.
BOB. Sorry I'm late. I, uh, had to give a lift to some people from work.
GROUP. Martini?
BOB. Make it a double. So how was your day?

(*At this cue the GROUP enters: five MEN and WOMEN wearing matching aprons. They are simultaneously describing the day he or she had. The MAN takes a martini from one and greets the others with hugs and kisses. This is all played as if it were routine, an everyday thing. Which, for these people, it is.*)

BOB. (*as the GROUP quiets*) So, what's for dinner.
GROUP. Thought we might hold off on dinner tonight.
SINGLE GROUP MEMBER (WOMAN #1). (*seductively*) I sent the kids to my mothers . . .
MEMBER (MAN #1). There's some white wine chilling.
MEMBER (MAN #3). Music?

(*Their voices overlap. The GROUP moves him to the chair. They try to get him in the "right mood".*)

MEMBER (WOMAN #3). Here, let me loosen that tie . . .
MEMBER (MAN #1). (*massaging his temples*) Ooo, you're so tense . . .

(*They are around him. Someone removes his shoes, another starts to unbutton his shirt. LIGHTS dim.*)

BOB. Wait. Not now. I'm really beat.

(*General response from the GROUP: More of the same.*)

BOB. No. My head is pounding.
GROUP. Oh?

(*MUSIC stops. LIGHTS come back up.*)

BOB. It was one thing after another all day. I didn't stop for a minute.

MEMBER (MAN #1). Oh didn't you?

(*There is a noticeable shift in tone.*)

BOB. Everything just seemed to pile up on me.

MEMBER (WOMAN #3). (*softly*) I'll bet they did.

GROUP. Humph!

BOB. What's that supposed to mean?

MEMBER (MAN #3). (*moving away*) Who'd you give a lift to today?

BOB. Just some people. People from work. Work people.

MEMBER (WOMAN #2). Why'd you have to take them home?

BOB. (*innocently*) They had flat tires.

MEMBER (MAN #1). All of them?

ANOTHER MEMBER (WOMAN #3). Whose earring is this? (*She produces an earring from her apron.*)

BOB. Where'd you get that?

MEMBER (WOMAN #1). Found it in the cuff of your pants.

BOB. (*at a loss*) It must have dropped there . . . while I was shopping or something.

MEMBER (MAN #3). I found this false eyelash stuck to your sweatsuit.

BOB. Well, I, um —

MEMBER (WOMAN #2). There was this contact lens on your bowling shirt.

MEMBER (WOMAN #1). (*holding up pen*) Whose T-ball jotter is this?

MEMBER (WOMAN #3). (*holding up socks*) Yesterday you came home wearing somebody else's socks. These are not your socks!

(*BOB searches for words and can find none. The GROUP lowers their evidence. Together:*)

GROUP. Who's Monique?

BOB. Why?

MEMBER (WOMAN #3). Last night in bed you cried for Monique.

BOB. Well —

MEMBER (MAN #3). Who's Sven?

MEMBER (WOMAN #1). Who's Yvonne?

ANOTHER MEMBER (MAN #1). Who are the Balducci Brothers?!

BOB. I can explain—

GROUP. Who are all the people in this picture?

(*They produce photo. They have him. He sits.*)

MEMBER (WOMAN #3). Can you imagine our humiliation? We were the last to know.

BOB. How did you find out?

MEMBER (WOMAN #1). (*twisting the knife*) We overheard at the Shop 'n Bag. It's common gossip. We had no idea.

BOB. I was going to tell you. (*There is a general reaction of disbelief.*) So what does all this mean?

GROUP. (*taking off their aprons*) We want out. (*They throw their aprons on the floor.*)

BOB. No. You can't. They don't mean anything to me.

MEMBER (MAN #3). We'll be by for the rest of our things in the morning, Bob.

BOB. Wait! (*The GROUP begins to move offstage.*) It was nothing! A chance meeting. Your ordinary group stuck in an elevator. Suddenly something clicked and Bang! It all happened so fast.

GROUP. Our mind's made up.

BOB. It was purely physical. I swear. That's all. Not like us.

MEMBER (WOMAN #3). If you need us we'll be at Mother's.

BOB. (*softly*) The bed'll be so empty without you.

GROUP. It'll be empty for us, too.

BOB. Alright, if that's what you want. (*Pause.*) I guess this is it.

GROUP. Guess so. . . . (*They start to move off.*)

BOB. Here's looking at you, Kids. (*They stop. Then continue grimly toward the door. There is much hesitation and shuffling of feet.*) Wait!

GROUP. What?!

BOB. (*a final plea*) We can't just throw away seven years like this. You mean everything to me. Please, don't leave me all alone.

GROUP. We don't want to leave you all alone!

BOB. Then don't!

GROUP. We just feel so . . .

BOB. I know. I know.

MEMBER (WOMAN #2). We don't know what you're doing all day.

ANOTHER MEMBER (MAN #1). And we never know when you're coming home anymore.

BOB. I know. I know.

MEMBER (MAN #3). We sit there, hour after hour, playing solitaire.

ANOTHER MEMBER (WOMAN #1). Waiting—

ANOTHER MEMBER (WOMAN #3).—and waiting.

BOB. It won't ever happen again.

GROUP. You promise?

BOB. I promise. Let's give it another try. What d'ya say, team? (*The GROUP is unsure.*) Who are my favorite Honeybears?

GROUP. (*melting*) Ooooohhhh . . .

[MUSIC NO. 12B]

(*They chase him offstage right as the MUSIC swells and the chair rolls off.*)

* * *

THE GUY I LOVE

[MUSIC NO. 13]

WOMAN #3 enters and sings.

WOMAN #3.
EVERY TIME I OPEN
THE CLASSIFIED SECTION,
SEEMS LIKE EVERYBODY'S HOPIN'
FOR ABSOLUTE PERFECTION.
BUT LOVE IS BUILT ON COMPROMISE
AND THAT COUNTS FOR ALOT,
SO WHEN YOU FIND THE ONE YOU LOVE
YOU WORK WITH WHAT YOU'VE GOT.
(*She calls offstage:*) Honey, hurry up! Song's starting!

(*A life-sized MR. POTATO HEAD enters and runs over to her.*)

Hi, sweetheart. Fix your tie. (*sings*)
THE GUY I LOVE
HAS A CROOKED GRIN,
(*She fixes his smile.*)
COULD LOSE SOME WEIGHT,
HASN'T GOT MUCH CHIN,
BUT I FELL FOR HIM LIKE THAT.
I LOVE EVERYTHING ABOUT THE GUY I LOVE
EXCEPT THAT HAT.
(*She removes his hat. Confused, he gropes about his head for it.*)
THE GUY I LOVE
KNOWS ME SO WELL,
DOESN'T SMOKE A PIPE,
KNOWS I HATE THE SMELL.
(*She takes the pipe out of his mouth.*)
LOVE'S A PIECE OF CAKE
WHEN THE GUY YOU LOVE KNOWS EVERYTHING IN
    LIFE
IS GIVE AND TAKE.
Give me your glasses. That way your eyes won't look so close together, honey.

(*She takes his glasses and moves his eyes to the far sides of his head. He attempts to move about the stage having only extremely peripheral vision.*)

NO ONE SAID RELATIONSHIPS WERE EASY.
(*MUSIC stops.*)
I just feel like all the romance has gone out of this relationship.
(*She moves his nose to where his crotch is.*)
That's better. (*She sings.*)
COMMITMENT DOESN'T COME WITHOUT A PRICE.
You never listen to me anymore, honey.
(*She rips off his ear and yells into it:*) Honey! (*She sings.*)
BUT WHEN I HAVE YOUR ARMS AROUND ME.
(*She puts his arms around her.*)
IT'S WORTH THE SACRIFICE.

(*She dances away, taking his arms with her. She takes a good look at him.*)

"THE GUY I LOVE"

THOSE WORDS SOUND STRANGE,
IT'S FUNNY HOW
A MAN CAN CHANGE.
(*picking up parts of him strewn about the stage*)
A HAT . . . A PIPE . . . A GLOVE . . .
THEY'RE SIMPLY MEMORIES OF
(*She looks at him again.*)
WHO ARE YOU?
WHAT HAPPENED TO
THE GUY I LOVE?

(*She dances off. Bewildered, he is left groping about the stage, bumping into walls, attempting to find his way out. He exits.*)

* * *

MICHAEL

KIM's chair and table move on from downstage R. *followed by KIM (WOMAN #2). She wears a bathrobe. It is late at night. She carries a telephone.*

VOICE-OVER. (*WOMAN #2 on tape, as the scene shifts*) M: Am I still your Sally Aardvark? Are you still my Many Men? -K.

(*KIM is imagining what she will say to the person on the other end of the phone. She speaks, trying his name different ways.*)

KIM. Hello, Michael . . . Hello, Michael . . . (*She tries to figure out what she will say.*) Hello, Michael . . . It's me . . . I just called to say "hi" . . . and to see how you're doing. I miss you. Goodbye . . . (*She hates this.* [MUSIC NO. 14] *She sings.*)
HELLO, MICHAEL
DID I WAKE YOU?
GUESS WHO SAW YOU:
EILEEN MITNER.
YOU LOOKED HAPPY,
SO SHE TOLD ME.
IF YOU'RE BUSY
I CAN CALL BACK.

WELL, I HAVE THIS
STUPID FAVOR,
YOU CAN REALLY
JUST SAY NO NOW
IF YOU WANT TO
YOU CAN REALLY
IF YOU WANT TO
JUST SAY NO.

YOU LOOKED HAPPY,
SO SHE TOLD ME,
BUT I WONDERED
DO YOU MISS ME?
DO YOU REALLY?
REALLY, REALLY?
MICHAEL, MISS ME?
DON'T YOU KNOW?
AM I STILL YOUR SALLY AARDVARK?
ARE YOU STILL MY MANY MEN?
AND I HAVE THIS STUPID FAVOR:
WOULD YOU MARRY ME AGAIN?
MICHAEL, MARRY ME AGAIN . . .

SO WHAT'S NEW THERE?
GUESS WHAT I DID.
STARTED DANCING.
SUCH A CLUTZY BALLERINA,
BUT I LIKE IT,
KEEPS ME BUSY.
I LOOK GREAT.
GUESS WHAT I'M LEARNING.
HOW TO COOK. YEAH.
OH, AND BABE, I
BOUGHT A BUNNY,
AND I NAMED IT AFTER YOU,
AND I CALL IT MANY MEN.

WELL, I'M LONELY.
GUESS YOU KNEW THAT.
AND I LOVE YOU.
REALLY, REALLY.
DO YOU CALL HER SALLY AARDVARK?

DOES SHE CALL YOU MANY MEN?
MICHAEL, MARRY ME.
MICHAEL, MARRY ME AGAIN.

MICHAEL, TELL ME WHY I LEFT YOU.
TELL ME WHAT I THOUGHT I WOULD FIND.
WHERE WAS I GOING? MICHAEL?
I WAS OUT OF MY MIND.

WELL I BLEW IT.
GUESS WE KNOW THAT.
AND I SEE NOW
IT WAS STUPID.
AND I'M SORRY,
GOD, I'M SORRY.
BUT I LOVE YOU.
CAN'T YOU SEE THAT?
CAN I COME HOME NOW?
WILL YOU TAKE ME?
MICHAEL, PLEASE, PLEASE,
PLEASE, JUST SAY "YES".
AM I STILL YOUR SALLY AARDVARK?
'CAUSE, BOY, YOU'RE STILL MY MANY MEN!
MICHAEL, MARRY ME,
MICHAEL, MARRY ME,
MICHAEL, MARRY ME,
MARRY ME,
MARRY ME, AGAIN.

(*She looks down at the phone.*)

MICHAEL . . .

(*She picks up the phone. Dials. Waits. She speaks.*)

KIM (*continued*) Hello? Michael? (*Pause.*) It's me. I just called to say "hi" . . . and to see how you're doing. I miss you. Good-bye.

(*She hangs up the phone. The LIGHTS fade on KIM, and she exits stage R. The platform rolls off downstage R.*)

* * *

MEETING SECTION

[MUSIC NO. 15]

*LIGHTS up on LOUIS, who crosses downstage center with his
table. Her nervously turns the tape on:*

TAPE (MAN #3). (*Beep*) Final check: I've been staring at you
from across the room. (*LOUIS repeats this line quickly under
his breath.*) I really like the look of you. (*LOUIS repeats it.*) I
was drawn to you like steel to a magnet. (*LOUIS repeats it.*)

(*CLAIRE enters and crosses downstage L.*)

CLAIRE. (*to herself, tying a scarf*) I can't believe I'm going out
with a man who would answer an ad in the paper. What am I doing?

TAPE (MAN #3). Reference points: Relationship. (*LOUIS
repeats it to himself.*) Commitment. (*LOUIS repeats it.*) Kahlua
Sombrero. (*LOUIS repeats it.*)

(*SAM enters and crosses downstage R.*)

SAM. (*to himself*) I can't believe I'm meeting a woman who
put an ad in the paper. What kind of a woman has to advertise in
the paper? I'll bet she's a troll.

TAPE (MAN #3). Well, Kid, this is it. How do you feel?
LOUIS. Great. I feel great. A little nervous, but—
TAPE. (*cutting him off*) Well you're as ready as you'll ever be.
The rest is up to you. Good luck. You are on your own.
(*Beeeeeep.*)

(*LOUIS stares at the recorder uneasily. CLAIRE, SAM and
LOUIS exit.*)

(*MUSIC begins, as the scene shifts to a bar. CLAIRE enters and
orders a drink. LOUIS enters. He musters his courage and
boldly crosses to WOMAN #2 who is seated at the bar.*)

LOUIS. Hello. My name is Louis. Would you have dinner with
me?

(*She has evidently heard this line a hundred times before. In fact, she completes it with him.*)

WOMAN #2. (*overlapping*) . . . have dinner with me.

(*Somewhat thrown, LOUIS turns to CLAIRE.*)

LOUIS. I've been staring at you from across the room, and I really like the look of you.

(*She also knows the routine.*)

CLAIRE. (*overlapping*) . . . really like the look of you.

(*In the face of all adversity, he gives it a final shot.*)

LOUIS. (*trying WOMAN #2 again*) I was drawn to you like steel to a magnet.
WOMAN #2. (*overlapping*) . . . like steel to a magnet.

(*Both WOMEN turn to him.*)

BOTH WOMEN. And you've never told anyone this before.
LOUIS. (*guilty*) And I've never told anyone this before. (*Beat.*) Thank you.

(*CLAIRE speaks to the audience:*)

CLAIRE. So, I'm on my second Absolut on the rocks with a splash and a twist waiting for "him" to show up, and all I can think is, if anyone catches me doing this I'll kill myself. (*SAM enters, and crosses to the bar.*) Just then, the cute guy from the apartment next to mine walks in. I consider performing Hari-Kiri on my swizzle stick.
SAM. (*to the audience*) I check out the bar. All I know is, I'm looking for someone who looks like they're looking for someone. (*He studies the bar.*) They *all* look like they're looking for someone. Then I see my next door neighbor. I consider a rush for the door. Too late. She sees me. What will she think when my troll shows up? (*He crosses to CLAIRE.*) Hello, there.
CLAIRE. Oh, hi. I almost didn't recognize you without groceries. (*They both laugh politely.*)

SAM. (*to the audience*) There is an awkward pause.

CLAIRE. I'm just waiting for a friend.

SAM. Me, too. (*She invites him to sit down. There is another long pause.*)

CLAIRE. (*to the audience*) Twenty minutes later . . . (*to SAM:*) So, did you ever get the Super to fix your dishwasher?

SAM. I have to get a new one.

CLAIRE. Don't hold your breath. (*They laugh. There is another painful pause.*)

SAM.(*to the audience*) By now, the inescapable reality of the situation has overwhelmed us.

CLAIRE. I attempt to figure out the odds against this happening. The mind boggles. (*They smile weakly at each other.*)

(*Shift to: LOUIS standing alone. As imaginary women go by him, he tries to approach them. WOMAN #2 exits.*)

LOUIS. Hello. My name is Louis. Would you . . . (*He clearly is ignored.*) Hello. My name is . . . Hello . . .

(*LOUISE [WOMAN #3] approaches LOUIS.*)

LOUISE. Hello. My name is Louise. Would you have dinner with me? (*LOUIS looks at her.*) I've been staring at you from across the room.

LOUIS. You have?

LOUISE. I really like the look of you.

LOUIS. You do?

LOUISE. I was drawn to you.

LOUIS. You were?

LOUISE. Let me buy you a drink. (*They sit at the bar.*)

(*Focus shifts to CLAIRE and SAM.*)

CLAIRE. (*to SAM*) No I'm not disappointed. I'm just surprised. The last thing I heard, you were moving in with this woman and you sublet your apartment to this French guy who used to steal my Sunday Times, and then he moves out and you move back, and I guess it didn't work out with her but frankly I don't want to know the details. (*to the audience:*) The vodka speaks for itself.

SAM. Well, I've got to tell you, I'm certainly seeing you in a different light.

CLAIRE. Oh?

SAM. All that stuff in your ad about "running in the rain" and "flying off to Paris". Well, it just sounds so . . . spontaneous.

CLAIRE. I don't seem spontaneous?

SAM. Well, I don't know . . . Did you ever notice how you fold your laundry? How you're so careful and precise, and if it isn't folded exactly right, how you'll unfold it and start all over again? Then there's all your little piles. You got your ankle socks, and your knee socks, and your stockings, and they're all arranged by color . . . (*CLAIRE does not seem pleased by this. SAM turns to the audience.*) I suddenly realize that my mouth is open and I am tasting feet.

(*Focus shifts to LOUIS and LOUISE. They are sitting close together.*)

LOUISE. Listen, Louis, I don't want you to think I usually do this on the first date, but you seem like a really nice guy. So let's cut the small talk and get right to the good stuff: let's skip to Lesson 14.

LOUIS. (*really thrown*) What? We can't do that. Lesson 14 is—

LOUISE. —is the best part.

LOUIS. Sure, but—

LOUISE. Then why wait?

LOUIS. Okay. Uh . . .

LOUISE. (*prompting*) Lesson 14.

LOUIS. Beep. (*They laugh at their inside joke. Then, just as he rehearsed it.*) Oh, Louise, these last three months together have been paradise.

LOUISE. And it's never been like this for me before, either.

LOUIS. And I've never loved anyone the way I love you . . . Louise. (*They begin to dance.*)

(*SAM and CLAIRE sit watching them.*)

CLAIRE. (*to the audience, gloomily*) We sit, staring at the young happy couple on the dance floor.

SAM. (*to the audience*) I feel the distance between us growing greater. I feel that I should say something. Do something. Instead, I spill something. (*He turns to her knocking his glass over.*) Oh, God, I'm sorry. Here. (*He offers his napkin.*)

CLAIRE. (*wiping her skirt*) That's okay. As we both know, I'm a whiz at laundry. So, should we call it here? Look for each other in the elevator and leave it at that?

SAM. No. We might as well at least have dinner together. (*CLAIRE hesitates.*) Come on, I want to hear all about how you "love to hang glide at dawn over the Rockies".

CLAIRE. Oh. That was a lie. I added it for color.

SAM. Ah. In that case, I think you should know I was never Ambassador to Luxembourg. (*She smiles and they start to leave.*)

CLAIRE. (*to the audience*) As we leave the bar, I am suddenly filled with an out-of-character Norman Rockwell sort of nostalgia as I realize I am out on a date with the boy next door. (*They exit.*)

(*The focus shifts to LOUIS and LOUISE. Lesson 14 is in full swing.*)

LOUIS. Oh, Louise, I never thought I could be this happy.

LOUISE. Louis, tonight let's make love like we've never made love before.

LOUIS. (*more to himself*) That shouldn't be difficult.

(*LOUIS and LOUISE dance off. The MUSIC ends. The LIGHTS fade as the bar is cleared.*)

* * *

PICKING UP LOUIS

LOUIS' table rolls on downstage L. LOUIS enters, seated in his chair. He is disheveled and appears very upset, but trying to contain it. He turns on the TAPE. We hear the recorded MUSIC. [MUSIC NO. 15A]

TAPE (MAN #3). Lesson 76. Picking Up the Pieces. How'd it go? (*Beep*)

LOUIS. (*snapping his fingers*) Like that. By the time we got back to her apartment we were up to Lesson 21, and by sunrise we were doing lesson 34, picking out names for our children. But the day went by so fast: Lesson 42, Lesson 51, lunch, Lesson 53. By the evening news we hit lesson 70: I was drinking heavily and she was telling me we were through. I gave that woman the 23 best hours of my life. I can't believe it's over.

(*There is a long pause. Then the TAPE begins to sing.*)

PICKING UP THE PIECES

[MUSIC NO. 16]

TAPE.
(*Beep*) HOW DO YOU FEEL?
    LOUIS. (*trying to be brave*) I feel okay. I feel—
    TAPE.
HOW DO YOU REALLY FEEL?
    LOUIS. I feel like I've grown.
    TAPE.
GET IT OUT.
TRY TO LET IT OUT.
DO YOU WANT TO CRY?
    LOUIS. No.
    TAPE.
COME ON, YOU WANT TO SCREAM AND CRY.
    LOUIS. I cried on the bus.
    TAPE.
BREAK A CUP.
GO THROW UP.
YOU'VE BEEN THROUGH HELL,
YOU'VE PAID YOUR DUES,
NOW THE NEXT STEP IS . . .
Lesson 77. Singing the Blues.

(*A music introduction is heard from the TAPE followed by a BEEP. LOUIS is confused and wary, but slowly he starts to sing.*)

    LOUIS.
I'VE BEEN HURT.
I FEEL BAD.
    TAPE.
(YEAH)

Louis.
I'VE BEEN DRAGGED THROUGH THE DIRT
OF LOVE,
AND I FEEL MAD,
AND I'VE BEEN HURT,
AND I DON'T LIKE IT.
    Tape.
(GET DOWN.)

(*He starts to get into this.*)

Louis.
I'M CONFUSED.
I FEEL NUMB.
I'VE BEEN BANGED UP AND BRUISED
BY LOVE,
AND I FEEL DUMB,
AND I FEEL USED,
AND I DON'T LIKE IT.

WHY
EVEN TRY,
IF YOU'RE ONLY GONNA END UP DODGING
    FLATWARE?
I WANNA DIE!
HOW COME IT HAS TO END LIKE THAT?! THERE,
THAT'S MY HEART
ON THE WALL.
IT'S BEEN HARPOONED BY THE DART
OF LOVE,
AND I FEEL SMALL,
AND RIPPED APART,
    Tape. (*spoken*) Take it home.
    Louis.
AND I DON'T EVER WANT TO GO THROUGH THAT
    AGAIN!

(*After a second, the TAPE sings again.*)

    Tape.
(*Beep*) DIDN'T THAT FEEL GOOD?
    Louis. It felt pretty good.

Tape.
DIDN'T THAT FEEL REALLY GOOD?
  Louis. It felt very good —
Tape.
OFF YOUR CHEST
AND WELL EXPRESSED.
NOW, SAY "IT'S IN THE PAST".
  Louis. (*trying*) It's in the past?
Tape.
SAY "IT'S IN THE DISTANT PAST".
  Louis. What?
Tape.
SAY "IT'S DEAD AND GONE",
  Louis. It was an hour ago —
Tape.
AND YOU'LL MOVE ON.
IT'S NOT SO HARD,
YOU'LL SEE THAT WHEN
YOU TAKE THE NEXT STEP . . .
(*Beep*) Lesson 78. Starting Your Life Again.

(*LOUIS stares at the TAPE in disbelief. He is appalled at the
    prospect of starting his life again.*)

  Louis.
BUT I'VE BEEN HURT.
  Tape (*fanfare*) Say "Today is the first day of the rest of my
life".
  Louis.
BUT I FEEL BAD.
  Tape. (*fanfare*) Now say it with a smile.
  Louis.
BUT I'VE BEEN DRAGGED THROUGH THE DIRT
OF LOVE,
AND I FEEL MAD.
  Tape. Say it like you mean it.
  Louis.
I'VE BEEN HURT!
  Tape. Right.
  Louis.
AND I DON'T LIKE THIS.
  Tape. Now, what are you going to do?

Louis.
I'LL STAY IN BED
 Tape. Good.
 Louis.
AND BE DEPRESSED.
 Tape. That's it.
 Louis.
SMOKE CIGARETTES, AND INSTEAD OF LOVE,
I'LL GET SOME REST.
 Tape. Okay!
 Louis.
UNTIL I'M DEAD!
 Tape.
NOW THAT'S MORE LIKE IT!

(*They sing together:*)

Tape.	Louis.
SOON,	
	WHAT?
VERY SOON	
	OH NO!
YOU'LL BE READY FOR ANOTHER LOVE	
	NO, DON'T SAY THAT.
MAYBE	
	WHAT?
TODAY	
	NO WAY!
YOU NEVER KNOW WHAT FATE MAY BR—	
	OKAY THAT'S IT!!

(*LOUIS shuts off the machine. There is a long pause. LOUIS sings to himself.*)

Louis.
IT'S JUST AS WELL
IT DIDN'T LAST.
SO WHAT IF I FELL
IN LOVE

AND HAD A BLAST,
I HURT LIKE HELL . . .

(*He stops, realizing.*)

I CAN'T BELIEVE I WANT TO GO THROUGH
THAT AGAIN.

(*LOUIS flips the tape and turns it on. The musical introduction is heard.*)

TAPE. Lesson One. (*Beep*)

(*Blackout.*)

* * *

SAM AND CLAIRE SCENE

[MUSIC NO. 16A]

Soft lights come up on CLAIRE's apartment. It is very late, around 5 a.m. CLAIRE is in her armchair, wrapped in a blanket. She is awake and appears to have been sitting there for quite some time. After a long pause, SAM enters. He is still half asleep. He is pulling on his pants and he carries his shirt. He sees her sitting in the chair and seems somewhat surprised at finding her there.

SAM. Hi. How long you been up?
CLAIRE. I never went to sleep.
SAM. You've been out here all night?
CLAIRE. Mmm hm.
SAM. Why?
CLAIRE. I knew that if I went to sleep, when I woke up it'd be tomorrow. And I didn't want to lose what was left of today. So I stayed up.
SAM. You should have woke me.
CLAIRE. (*with a smile*) I tried.
SAM. Sorry.

(*SAM leans down and they kiss. He begins to put his shirt on.*)

CLAIRE. You leaving?

SAM. No. I'm freezing. Do you want me to leave?

CLAIRE. No.

SAM. Then I'm not.

CLAIRE. Okay. So, how does it feel to be dating the girl next door?

SAM. (*gently teasing*) It has been great. No rushing across town at six a.m. to get changed for work. No heavy decision about "your place or mine". And whenever we want to see each other, we can just bang on the wall or yell through the vent in the kitchen. What do you think?

CLAIRE. What happens if we have a fight?

SAM. I guess we bang harder and yell louder. What's wrong? I'm having a great time with you, and I could keep having a great time, but if I'm the only one having a great time, sooner or later I'm gonna feel pretty dumb. So . . .

CLAIRE. (*turning to him*) You know how when you really fall for someone, how you get this . . . this feeling inside you like . . . like you've got a . . . little bird in here and it's trying to fly out? Well, Sam, you give me birds.

SAM. Thank you.

CLAIRE. And that's why I don't think we should see each other anymore.

SAM. Whoa, go back.

CLAIRE. We live next door to each other. After we break up I won't want to see you bringing someone else home and hear the two of you singing in the shower or even ride down in the elevator with you and have nothing to say. And, Sam, this building is going co-op and I don't want to have to move.

SAM. Wait a minute. Why are we breaking up?

CLAIRE. Have you ever been involved with someone where you didn't break up?

SAM. (*thinks*) No.

CLAIRE. So let's walk away while it's still wonderful. Let's call it quits before things start to go wrong. Before it starts to not work out. Before all I've got left are a lot of dead birds.

SAM. Claire, what makes you think it's gonna be any easier breaking it off now? I'm still gonna want you every time I see you in the compactor room tying up your old newspapers into those neat little bundles. Am I crazy? This is good, right?

CLAIRE. Right, but—

SAM. No "buts". Good is good. I've spent an awful long time waiting for "good". I like it. You like it?

CLAIRE. So far.

SAM. Good. Then I'm sorry, but I'm not going anywhere.

CLAIRE. Good.

SAM. We're just going to have to wait and see.

CLAIRE. I hate "wait and see". I hate "giving it time" and "trusting it".

SAM. It's gonna be all right.

CLAIRE. I hate that too.

SAM. Come on. What do you say? (*He kisses her.*) Hey, you wanna go feed the birds? (*They kiss again.*)

SOME THINGS DON'T END

[MUSIC NO. 17]

As the kiss continues, the set clears and the other FOUR enter upstage and sing.

WOMAN #2.
SOME THINGS ARE DOOMED
RIGHT FROM THE TOP.
WOMAN #2, #3.
FROM THE WORD "GO"
YOU HEAR THE WORD "STOP."
WOMAN #2, #3, MAN #2, #3.
SOME THINGS THERE'S REALLY
NO WAY TO DEFEND.
ALL.
BUT SOMETIMES
SOME THINGS DON'T END.

I FIND SOMEONE NEW
THEY QUICKLY GET OLD.
SOMEONE TO HAVE
NOT SOMEONE TO HOLD.
I START WITH A LOVER
WIND UP WITH A FRIEND
BUT SOMETIMES
SOME THINGS DON'T END.

I THINK MY CHANCES OF FINDING YOU
ARE SOMEWHERE FROM SLIM TO NONE.

THEN OUT OF THE BLUE
YOU FALL INTO MY LIFE
AND I KNOW THAT THE HARD PART HAS ONLY
  BEGUN.

I HOLD YOU TOO TIGHT.
I FORCE YOU AWAY.
I'M SCARED THAT YOU'LL LEAVE.
I'M SCARED THAT YOU'LL STAY.
BUT WE'LL WORK AND WE'LL PRAY
AND WE'LL LEARN HOW TO BEND
SO THAT THIS TIME
SOMETHING
MAYBE THIS TIME
SOMETHING
I KNOW THAT SOME TIMES
SOME THINGS . . .
  ALL. (*variously*)
DON'T END
DON'T END
DON'T END
DON'T END
DON'T END
DON'T END
DON'T END
DON'T END
DON'T END
DON'T END
DON'T END
DON'T END

END ACT TWO

* * *

[MUSIC NO. 18: BOWS]

CURTAIN CALLS

  ALL.
. . . AND I KNOW THERE'S SOMEONE OUT THERE
WAITING SOMEWHERE IN THE NIGHT

SOMEONE WAITING FOR MY FIFTEEN WORDS
TO LIGHT UP THE BLACK AND WHITE,
AND I THINK THIS TIME I FINALLY GOT IT RIGHT!

END OF SHOW

(*While the audience is leaving the theatre, a slide is projected:*)

"C.B.: I'm coming back. — Boop."

PROP PLOT

ACT ONE

Nothing To Do With Love
Five chairs
Magazine
Clipboard
Two newspapers
Yellow pad
Pencil

Typesetter 1
Chair
Desk
Typewriter
Lamp
Visor
Index cards
"In-Out" tray

Woman Seeks
Clipboard

Typesetter 2
Same as *Typesetter 1*

Mama's Boys
Phone receiver and cord
Game table with mah jong tiles
Three chairs
Microphone on stand

Videomatch — Tina
Chair
Clipboard
Three index cards

Louis 1
Table
Cassette recorder with tape
Pencil
Notepad

A Night Alone
Chair
T.V. cart
T.V.
Bottle of scotch
Clock
Telephone
Book
Dust bunny
Blender
Tuna souffle dish
Lamp
Ficas leaf

Videomatch — Ricki
Chair

Louis 2
Same as *Louis 1*

I Think You Should Know
Loveseat
Chair
Table
Answering machine
Telephone

Typesetter 3
Chair
Wallet with photos
Beer

Videomatch — Hannah
Chair

Second Grade
Three beer mugs
Washing machine
Paperback book
Bottle of detergent
Table
Two chairs

Two napkins
Three pieces of luggage
Squirt gun

Louis 3
Same as *Louis 1* — Add Chair

Imagine My Surprise
Clipboard
Bench

Dance Alone
Six Manniquins

ACT TWO

Moving In With Linda
Tray
Crock pot
Casserole dish
Baggie twistems
Handtruck
Three boxes — one large enough to contain Woman #1
Trunk
Garment rack
Two garment bags
Shirt
Plaster bust
Fan
Pompon
Phone receiver

A Little Happiness
Same as *Typesetter 1* — add tin with cookies

Kim's Monologue
Pregnant manniquin

I Could Always Go To You
Two stools

Group
Chair

Slippers
Martini
T-Ball jotter
Earring
Socks
Photograph
Briefcase

Michael
Same as *I Think You Should Know*, without loveseat

The Meeting Section
Louis' table with:
    Notepad
    Pencil
    Cassette Recorder
    Kahlua Sombrero
Table
Two chairs
Plastic rocks glass with swizel stick
Bar
Five bar stools
Dish rag
Three beer mugs
Bar bottle
Bar rag
Two rocks glasses
Paper napkin

Picking Up The Pieces
Same as *Louis 3*

Sam and Claire Scene
Chair
Afgan
Lamp

COSTUME PLOT

CLAIRE/WOMAN 1

Nothing To Do With Love
Blouse
Tweed vest
Paisley flaired skirt
Pumps

Mama's Boys
Pink Chanel suit
Suede belt
Scarf

VideoMatch — Tina
Same as *Nothing To Do With Love*

A Night Alone
3/4 length capri pants
Blouse
Jacket
Flat tie shoes

Videomatch — Ricki
Same as *Night Alone*, change jacket for vest

Videomatch — Hannah
Skirt, same as *Opening*
Blouse

Second Grade
Pink silk kimono
Scarf
Heels

Imagine My Surprise
Sweater
Skirt, same as opening
Pumps
Scarf

Dance Alone
Same as *Second Grade*, add jeweled belt

Moving in with Linda
Letter sweater
Pleated skirt
White blouse
Cable knee socks
Tennis shoes with yarn pompons
Head band

Always Go To You
Wool sweater
Straight skirt
Pumps

Group
Same as *Always Go To You*, add full body orange apron

Meeting Section
Same as Opening, add clutch purse

Sam and Claire Scene
Same as *A Night Alone*, without jacket

Finale
Same as *Sam and Claire Scene*

KIM/WOMAN 2

Nothing To Do With Love
Blue and green striped cotton blouse
Diamond patterned sweater
Light weight overvest
Cuffed pants
High top sneakers

Woman Seeks
Same as *Opening*, without sweater

Mama's Boys
Light blue tunic

Light blue stretch pants
Leg warmers
Flat suede boots

I Think You Should Know
Blouse, Same as *Opening*
Diamond patterned sweater vest
Leather belt
Denim mini skirt
Textured hose
Pumps

Second Grade
Grey wool overcoat
High heeled boots

Dance Alone
Same as *Mama's Boys*

Moving In With Linda
Suede moccasins
Bell bottom blue jeans
Indian cotton shirt
Suede fringe vest
Bandana headband

Kim's Monologue
Same as *Opening*, add hat and purse

Group
Blue cotton crop top
Stretch pants
Orange French maids apron
Pumps

Michael
Blue chenille full length bathrobe
Bedroom slippers

The Meeting Section
Light blue silk dress
High heel pumps
Shoulder purse

Some Things Don't End
Same as *Opening*

LOUISE/WOMAN 3

Nothing To Do With Love
Baggy plaid green overalls
Gold V-neck blouse
Tie
Tie shoes

Mama's Boys
Blue knit dress
Cobby shoes
Wig

Videomatch — Tina
Business suit with conservative jacket and straight skirt
White blouse
Glasses
Tennis shoes and socks

Videomatch — Ricki
Gold patterned sweatshirt
Print jeans
Leather jacket

Videomatch — Hannah
Black skirt
Black shirt
Black vest

Second Grade
Cotton blouse
Flowered cotton skirt
Sandals

Dance Alone
Peach jersey jumpsuit
Wide white belt
Ankle boots

Moving in With Linda
Gold evening gown
High heels

Always Go To You
Wool sweater
Pleated skirt
Pumps

Group
Same as *Always Go To You*, add orange full body apron

The Guy I Love
Same as *Always Go To You*, add frilly full body apron

Meeting Section
Cream blouse with big bow at the neck
Pleated skirt
Loafers

Finale
Same as *Opening*

SAM/MAN 1

Nothing To Do With Love
Green plaid flannel shirt
Blue jeans
Brown leather belt
Denim jacket
Top siders

Woman Seeks
Off white boat neck shirt
Light colored striped sports jacket
Light grey slacks
Grey loafers

Mama's Boys
Blue lace dress
Mink stole

Stockings to knee
Black sandels
Woman's wig

A Night Alone
Same as *Opening*, without denim jacket

I Think You Should Know
Grey "slinky" shirt
Suit style vest
Grey slacks

Second Grade
Three piece grey suit
Tie
Loafers

Dance Alone
Same as *Woman Seeks*, without jacket

Moving In With Linda
Blue plaid flannel shirt
Dark tweed jacket
Blue jeans
Black loafers

Group
Same as *Dance Alone*, add orange bar-b-que apron

Meeting Section
Blue plaid flannel shirt
Green tweed slacks
Dark tweed jacket
Scarf

Sam and Claire Scene
Same as *Night Alone*

Finale
Same as *Night Alone*

LOUIS/MAN 2

Nothing To Do With Love
Brown-rust shirt
4-in-hand tie
Dark green corduroy pants
Cardigan sweater vest
Leather/Suede saddle shoes
Glasses

After School Special
Sweat shirt
Old letter jacket
Baseball cap
Worn jeans
Knee pads
Tennis shoes

Woman Seeks
Sports jacket with patches on sleeves
Snap down cap
Shirt
Light argyle sweater vest
Light brown slacks

Mama's Boys
Shirtwaist dress with bib apron
Stockings to knee
Black sandels
Woman's wig

Louis 1
Same as *Opening*, exchange green corduroy pants for baggy
    patterned corduroy green pants

Louis 2
Same as *Louis 1*

Second Grade
Light brown corduroy sports jacket
Turtleneck sweater
Light brown slacks

Louis 3
Same as *Louis 1*, without vest

Dance Alone
Same shirt and slacks from *Woman Seeks*

Moving in With Linda
Light blue denim coveralls and cap
Burgandy coveralls and cap
Lavender coveralls and cap
Black work boots

Group
Light brown business suit
Conservative shirt
Tie
Handkerchief
Loafers, change to slippers

The Guy I Love
Mr. Potato Head Costume with Detachable:
    Pipe
    Hat
    Mouth
    Glasses
    Eyes
    Nose
    Ear
    Hands

The Meeting Section
Same as *Louis 1*, exchange sweater vest for sports jacket

Picking Up The Pieces
Same as *Louis 1*, without tie

Finale
Same as *Opening*

TYPESETTER/MAN 3

Nothing To Do With Love
Brownish slacks

Window pane plaid dress shirt
Cardigan sweater
4-in-hand tie
Loafers

Typesetter 1
Same as *Opening*, add visor

Woman Seeks
Short sleeved shirt with double pockets
Tie
Panama hat
Sunglasses
Same slacks from *Opening*

Typesetter 2
Same as *Typesetter 1*, add overcoat

Mama's Boys
Striped collarless shirt
Light blue pants with narrow suspenders

A Night Alone
Khaki trench coat
Plaid scarf

Typesetter 3
Same as *Typesetter 1*, without sweater

Second Grade
Shirt
Muted tweed jacket
Light slacks
Loafers
Ascot

Dance Alone
Same as *Second Grade*, exchange jacket for cotton cardigan
    sweater vest

Moving in with Linda
Light blue denim coveralls and cap
Burgandy coveralls and cap

Lavender coveralls and cap
Black work boots

A Little Happiness
Same as *Typesetter 1*

Group
Shirt and slacks from *Second Grade*
Orange chef's hat
Orange short waiters apron

Meeting Section
Shirt and Slacks from *Second Grade*
Bib Bartenders Apron
Bow Tie

Finale
Same as *Opening*

DAVID CRANE (Author/Lyrics) has had musical and sketch material in the Off-Broadway revues "Martin Charnin's Upstairs at O'Neals'" and "A...My Name is Alice" at the Village Gate, as well as the CBS series "The Comedy Zone." He is co-author with Larry Coen of "Epic Proportions," produced by the Manhattan Punch Line Theatre, and co-author/lyricist of "Rapunzel" for Theatreworks/ USA. David received an Outer Critics Circle Award and a Drama Desk Award nomination for his work on "Personals" as well as several ASCAP awards.

SETH FRIEDMAN (Author/Composer/Lyrics) is an alumnus of the New York University musical theatre program, where he worked with Arthur Laurents, Leonard Bernstein, Stephen Schwartz and Martin Charnin. He composed the music and co-wrote the lyrics for material in "Martin Charnin's Upstairs at O'Neals'" and has written for the CBS-TV series "The Comedy Zone." He is coauthor of "Stars & Stripes," a screenplay for MGM/UA, and has received several ASCAP awards.

MARTA KAUFFMAN (Author/Lyrics) has had material in the Off-Broadway revues "A...My Name is Alice" and "Martin Charnin's Upstairs at O'Neals'" on which she assisted Mr. Charnin. Marta is co-author/lyricist of "Rapunzel." She is a recipient of several ASCAP awards, an Outer Critic's Circle Award, the Brandeis Alumni Achievement Award for musical theatre, and a Drama Desk Award nomination. She also wrote "Arthur, the Musical" with Michael Skloff and David Crane.

WILLIAM DRESKIN (Composer) studied music at Brandeis University where he wrote the score for "Waiting for the Feeling" (which, like "Personals" was also produced at the Kennedy Center as part of the American College Theatre Festival.) He writes (and appears with) Beged Kefet, a group of musicians who perform solely to benefit charitable organizations. "Personals" marks his off-Broadway debut and coincides with the completion of his rabbinical studies at the Hebrew Union College of New York.

JOEL PHILLIP FRIEDMAN (Composer) is a graduate of Boston University, where he won the Malloy Miller memorial composition prize for his song cycle "One Evening's Poems." He studied conducting with Dr. Robert Sirota and composition with Theodore Antoniou, Joyce Mekeel and David del Tredici. He has had works commissioned by the American Saxophone Project and the Boston Wind Quintet. Joel is also a freelance editor/music copyist for Leonard Bernstein and others.

ALAN MENKEN (Composer) composed the score for the award-winning musical "Little Shop of Horrors" and the hit movie of the same name. Other musicals include: "Goodbye, Mr. Rosewater," "Real Life Funnies," "Patch, Patch Patch," and "Atina: Evil Queen of the Galaxy." Along with lyricist Howard Ashman, he also wrote songs for "The Little Mermaid," a Walt Disney animated feature. He is a recipient of the BMI career achievement award.

STEPHEN SCHWARTZ (Composer) wrote the music and lyrics for "Godspell," "Pippin," "The Magic Show," "The Baker's Wife," four of the songs for "Working," and the title song for "Butterflies are Free." For children, he has written a one-act musical, "The Trip." Most recently, he has written the lyrics for "Rags."

MICHAEL SKLOFF (Composer) composed music for the Off-Broadway hit "A...My Name is Alice." He composed the score for the musical "Rapunzel" for Theatreworks/USA and he is currently working on the musical "Arthur" with Marta Kauffman and David Crane. Michael has been nominated for Outer Critics Circle Awards and is the recipient of several ASCAP musical theatre awards.

SAMUELFRENCH.COMS

www.ingramcontent.com/pod-product-compliance
Lightning Source LLC
Chambersburg PA
CBHW070635120726
47909CB00004B/1452